By the same author

AN AGE
HOTHOUSE
THE SALIVA TREE
BEST SCIENCE FICTION STORIES OF BRIAN W. ALDISS
EARTHWORKS
NON-STOP
GREYBEARD
THE DARK LIGHT YEARS
THE AIRS OF EARTH
THE CANOPY OF TIME
CITIES AND STONES: A Traveller's Juguslavia

Edited by the author
INTRODUCING SF

Report on Probability A

Report on Probability A

Brian W. Aldiss

Doubleday & Company, Inc./Garden City, New York/1969

For Mike Moorcock

I think you were in the darkness of the garden
If there was a voice I think you heard it
And if neither knows what communication is
We agree on the cost of garden produce

Do not, I beg you, look for
anything behind phenomena. They
are themselves their own lesson.

Goethe

Report on Probability A

Part One

G Who Waits

1

The Report begins:

One afternoon early in a certain January, the weather showed a lack of character. There was no frost or wind; the trees in the garden did not stir. There was no rain, although anybody accustomed to predicting rain might have forecast it with a fair expectation of being right before nightfall. Cloud lay thickly over the sky. The face of the sun was not visible. Consequently, shadows had no form.

A single window on the north-west side of the house reflected the light back in a dull fashion, without movement, except once when the reflection of a pigeon, wheeling above the garden, splashed across it. No movement came from the house. No sound came from the house.

G lived not in the house but in a wooden bungalow in the garden, overlooked by the window set high in the north-west side of the house. The bungalow, which contained only one room, measured about five by four metres, being longer than it was deep. It was raised above the ground on low pillars of brick. It was constructed of planks arranged vertically on the front and rear and horizontally on the sides. Its roof was also of planks, covered by asphalt; the asphalt was secured in place by large flat-headed nails which dug into the black material. Cracks ran round many of the nails.

The wooden bungalow had two windows. These were fitted in its front wall, one on either side of a door. This was the only door. It did not fit well. The windows contained large single panes of glass. The window-frames and the door had been painted with white paint. Although dirt had greyed this paint, it was still in moderately good condition and not in particular need for repainting. The rest of the wooden bungalow, excluding of course the roof, had been painted yellow. This paint had proved less satisfactory than the white, peeling off in many places to reveal the bare wood underneath.

Between the two windows was an ill-fitting door. A key remained in the lock of this door on the inside, although the lock would not function because the door hinges had sunk and the wood had swollen. G always shut this door with great force at night; he did not like to imagine that Mr. Mary might enter the wooden bungalow when he was inside it asleep. Sometimes when G shut the door with great force at night, the key would fall out of the lock onto the mat.

Approximately two years had passed since G began

living in the wooden bungalow. During that period, the key had fallen onto the mat inside the door on many occasions.

When Mr. Mary had had men build the wooden bungalow in the garden, he said to his wife: 'It is for you; you can call it your summer house.' The wooden bungalow had been constructed facing the north-west side of the house. It did not face it squarely, but at an angle of some twenty degrees, in the direction of east-south-east. It stood at a distance of some ten metres from the house. The house dominated the wooden bungalow.

On the early January days when the sun shone, it never rose far enough above the roof of the house to illuminate more than the upper half of the two windows on the front of the bungalow. Even this ration of sunshine was further abbreviated while the shadow of a group of chimneys on the roof of the house made its passage across the front of the bungalow. Since the bungalow faced east-south-east, the sunshine that did reach the windows impinged obliquely into the one room. It shone onto a small section of mat that was stretched over the floorboards and over a portion of the couch on which G slept. G was never on the couch when the sun was.

The couch stood along the northmost side of the room. At the other end of the room to the couch, G had a small stove of an antique pattern which burnt paraffin. By this stove was a chair on which G sat for a considerable period each day. One of the rear legs of this chair was slightly shorter than the others, so that it was possible to make the chair rock a little when one wished it to do so. The chair had once belonged in the house. The style of the chair was the style known to G as wheelback, because the spokes that formed the back of the chair radiated out from a centre in a fashion reminiscent of the hubs of a cart wheel. The back of the chair had once possessed five supports or spokes; one of these spokes had been missing for a long time. It was because this spoke was missing that Mr. Mary had ordered the chair to be placed in the wooden bungalow. The chair had been made shortly before the first world war; it bore on the underside of the round wooden seat the date 1912. G had seen this date and did not forget it.

When G sat on the chair, he generally permitted his gaze to rest only on the objects inside the bungalow. These objects were few in number. He was familiar with all of them. Most of the objects were manufactured, as were a stove with a pattern of circular holes on its upper surface and a galvanized bucket that stood near the chair. Most of them had not been intended originally for the wooden bungalow, but had been brought over from the house by Mr. Mary; some had been brought over by his wife, before they had quarrelled. One or two belonged to G.

Some of these objects were connected directly or in a more tenuous degree with the passage of time. G's clock had been specifically designed to indicate the passage of time; it was his clock, for he had bought it with part of his wages in the days when Mr. Mary was paying him a weekly fee. On its face, which formed a circle, were the arabic numerals from one to twelve and a pair of hands. The smaller of the two hands pointed at the lower lobe of the figure eight, while the larger hand pointed at the space between the nine and the ten. These two hands had been at these positions, maintaining between them an angle of fifty degrees, for a period of something over eleven months. Although, when his attention encompassed the clock, G entertained the theory that the clock still worked, he was reluctant to test the theory by attempting to wind the clock mechanism.

Also connected with the passage of time was a calendar for the previous year, 19—. It indicated the day as being 9th February. G was aware that this date was incorrect. Above the functional part of the calendar (non-functioning though it was) hung a picture, stuck to the same piece of cardboard that bore the pack of dates. When G turned his attention to it, he saw that it bore a representation of two men in period dress standing on the edge of a gorge. One of these men wore a black beard and was pointing with a stick into the gorge; the other man held his hat in his hand and seemed to be gazing, not into the gorge, but at the end of the bearded man's stick. In the foreground of the picture, the gorge was littered by broken trees and boughs and boulders of large dimension. In the distance, the gorge became purple; over this end of it, a bird with a large wingspan hovered. The scene, though grand, was not harsh, because a gentle afternoon light played across it. This light bathed the two men as if from the wings of a theatre, giving them an air of security although they stood so close to a precipice.

A third object connected more remotely with the passage of time was the front page of a daily newspaper, The Daily ——, for a day in April of the preceding year. G had fastened this sheet of newsprint and pictures to the wooden wall by two drawing pins, one at each of the two top corners of the paper; later he had added two more drawing pins at the bottom corners, because the damp emanating from the wall had caused the paper to curl upwards.

G had kept this sheet of newspaper because he found its contents more interesting than the contents of most newspapers. The main headline across the page said SERIOUS BLAZE DAMAGES WARSHIP IN SOUTHERN HARBOUR. The report of this fire, in which nobody was injured, was illustrated by an aerial photograph of the warship with smoke pouring from it. When G was a child of seven years, an uncle had taken him to see this ship. On the other side of the page, headlines announced ZEGENGAIS UNDER ARREST. In the last column was a notice of a strike in a car factory. Lower down the page were items of more domestic interest: MITZI TABORI WEDS FOURTH HUSBAND, FISH FAMINE CAUSES RECORD PRICES, and a report on a day of a big murder trial headed 'IN LAUGHING FIT I KILLED HER'. An item which particularly interested G as a gardener was headed HOSE GOES!, and described how a man in the state of New York had watched in amazement while his fifty-feet-long garden hose had burrowed underground, resisting everyone's attempts to pull it back; it had finally disappeared, only to reappear two days later outside the Baptist church in what was described as a dazed condition.

Between the sheet of newspaper, which hung on one of the side walls, and the wheelback chair, stood a galvanized bucket and a paraffin stove of old-fashioned design. A small table made of bamboo stood on the other side of the wheelback chair, nearer the couch.

Also in the room was a cupboard of unpainted wood, in which G kept several small toilet articles; a copy of Hugh Walpole's 'The Cathedral'; some neatly folded bandages; a crumpled handkerchief belonging to Mr. Mary's wife; a bowl with a rose pattern in which lay rusting curtain hooks, a penknife, and a pair of spectacles that had belonged to an uncle of G's; a candlestick; some candles; string; several strangely shaped stones found in the garden; a white china cat with the name of a seaside town printed on its stomach; some mending things; a round 1 oz. tobacco tin with holes punched in its lid, in which G had once intended to keep a lizard; and some groceries.

To the left of the cupboard of unpainted wood was one of the two windows set in the front wall of the wooden bungalow. Attached to the left side of it, as G sat on his seat regarding it, was a mirror measuring some fifteen by thirty centimetres and framed in a veneered wood, such as might have belonged at some past period to a small version of a cheval-glass. This mirror or looking-glass was fixed to the window frame at such an angle that, as G sat on the wheelback chair, he could look at the mirror and see reflected in it a part of the garden not otherwise visible from where he sat.

This was the part of the garden visible when one overlooked it in a southerly direction. The reflection showed the west corner of the house, with a concrete path leading round it; and certain limited sections of the garden, such as the vegetable garden, the fruit garden, and a narrow section of a long lawn on which trees grew, beyond which lay, hidden by the decline of the ground, a sunken garden; these sections were divided from each other by privet hedges running in various directions, chopped into pieces by the narrow dimensions of the looking-glass, so that the true relationship of the pieces to one another, the fact that they were often merely fragments of one hedge, would have been lost to a newcomer looking into the mirror.

The hypothetical newcomer would also have seen a more distant hedge that divided the garden from the property of an elderly bachelor known to have an ancestor who had built a lighthouse in the southern hemisphere; part of an asparagus bed lying between the back of the house and an old brick outhouse; the old brick outhouse itself, on the roof of which strutted a homing pigeon; a round window set in the front of the brick building; and sundry other particulars that were regularly glimpsed by G when he directed his gaze to the mirror. Most of the time he sat looking directly out of the window, staring at the blank wall of the house some distance away or, for preference, staring down comfortably at the floor.

On the floor lay two old fibre mats, the stripes of which had faded from their original oranges and greens under the long application of human feet. Because it was not raining, G took up one of these mats and carried it outside. As he began to shake it, he saw Mr. Mary's wife come round the edge of the house. She was walking from the back door to the side gate, which meant that she had to traverse the length of path between G and the house, coming at her nearest point to within twenty metres of him; she saw him, and he knew she saw.

He continued to flap the mat before him, so that its faded orange and green stripes rose and fell before his vision, alternately revealing and concealing her; between each brief concealment she was a fraction further along the path.

When she was at perihelion, and already only a few metres from the brown side gate, G let his arms drop and faced her through the cloud of dust that hung in the air between them.

'When the fishing is poor, they say the price of fish rises.'

'Fish are plentiful now.'

'Are the fish eager to be caught?'

'My fishmonger has satisfied customers all the year.'

'Even in a time of plenty, are not some fish more satisfying than others?'

'All fish contain vitamin, so says my fishmonger.'

Although she slowed her pace as she spoke, Mr. Mary's wife never entirely stopped walking towards the brown side gate; nor did she entirely turn her face towards G. She had now reached the brown side gate, and turned her attention to the bolt. Shedding a small flake of rust, it yielded, and she swung the gate open. She walked through it and closed it from the outside. The gate was set in a wall nearly two metres high; on the top of the wall were embedded a few shreds of bottle glass.

Domoladossa looked up from the long report.

'Mr. Mary's wife,' he said. 'We think she may be the key to the whole matter. I shall be interested to see what the report makes of her.'

'The main object of the report is directed towards a different objective,' Midlakemela said. 'Let us call this continuum we are studying—the one containing Mr. Mary

and his wife—Probability A. We know it is closely related to our continuum, which I like to think of as Certainty X. Nevertheless, even superficially, Probability A reveals certain basic values that differ widely from our own. It is our first duty to examine those values.'

Domoladossa sighed. He both admired and detested the slow, careful mind of the younger man.

'Quite so. Probability A's time-flow rate seems to differ from our own, for instance. Instrumentation is being devised so that we can have absolute scales by which to measure such discrepancies.' He looked askance at Midlakemela. 'Has it occurred to you that our congruence with Probability A may be temporary? In a week it may have vanished again.'

'And then?'

'We may be left all alone in the uni-probable space-time universe familiar to our fathers. Or the faulting may occur again, and we may find ourselves congruent with Probability Z, where few factors indeed coincide with our own. We just don't know.'

'So perhaps we should continue to peruse the report.' Midlakemela was the sort who always got promotion.

There was neither frost nor wind that afternoon. The trees in the garden did not stir. Behind the wooden bungalow was a long brick wall marking the north-west boundary of the garden; beech trees were planted beside it from the bottom of the garden to a point not far from the wooden hut, where an elder tree incongruously stood, its lax branches touching the back of the wooden bungalow; these trees did not stir. On the side of the house

24

facing the wooden bungalow, only one window looked out, a high bow window, set near the east or street corner of the house; a curtain stirred at this window.

G looked quickly up and caught the movement of the curtain. He could not see anybody at the window. The curtain was of a cream material. It did not move again. G covered his mouth momentarily with his hand and then rubbed it. He turned away and took the striped mat back into the wooden bungalow. He deposited the mat back on the floor of the bungalow. Then he emerged into the open once again, carrying the second mat. He commenced to shake this as thoroughly as he had shaken the first one. A cloud of dust rose in the air before him. As he worked, he kept his eye on the bow window set high in the blank wall of the house.

A black and white cat picked its way daintily through the stems of a privet bush that bounded the lawn to his left hand. It held its tail erect. It walked past a sundial that was supported by an almost naked boy cast in iron, rubbing against the boy's legs as it went, heading towards G. G ceased to shake the rug. He called to the cat in an affectionate tone. The cat made a noise in reply.

G retreated into the wooden bungalow, carrying a striped mat which he laid on the floor in a convenient position, next to a second and similar mat. Straightening his back, he moved over to a cupboard of unpainted wood, opened one of its doors, and extracted from its shelves a small white jug of the kind generally used for keeping milk in. G went to the door and showed this jug to the cat. The cat climbed up the step of the wooden bungalow and rubbed himself against the door.

'You're early for your rations today. The jug's empty till I get some more, but you'd better come in.'

The cat entered the wooden bungalow, crossed the floor, and jumped up onto the couch. G closed the door, pressing his shoulder to it to do so. He returned the white jug to the cupboard, leaving one of the cupboard doors open. Then he went over to the couch and picked up the cat round its chest, so that its paws hung down, black and white in varying proportions.

'You're a naughty pussy cat. What's she been doing today? Where do you think she's going, eh?'

He carried the cat over to the wheelback chair and sat down facing the window that had a mirror attached to it. He arranged the cat on his lap; the cat settled itself. It purred. It had a white tip to its tail.

'You'll never tell me, will you? You never tell me a thing.'

G stroked the cat. His hands were thick. He did not look at the cat. He looked out of the two windows, his gaze moving from the left one to the right one. Looking through the left one, he could see the front wall of the garden, but not the brown side gate that was set in it. Finally Mr. Mary's wife appeared, visible through the left window, walking along the concrete path that ran from the side gate, round the back of the house, to the back door. She was looking straight ahead.

She walked along the path. She was invisible for a moment, hidden from view of the left window, and then she could be seen through the right-hand window. The view of her was now rather less of a side view than a half-back view. She became hidden by the side of the window frame. G leaned forward, so that the black and

26

white cat stuck its claws through his trousers and into his thighs. The woman now appeared reflected in the mirror set slantwise against the side of the window. She presented an almost full back view, walking towards the corner of the house. Her coat could be inspected, and her brown hair above her coat. She moved round the side of the house and was gone. The mirror reflected only a portion of the garden.

G sat up straight again. He removed the cat's claws, unhooking them gently from his trousers. He cleared his throat. He began to stroke the animal again.

2

When the rain began that afternoon, the time by the hands of G's clock was almost ten minutes to eight.

The rain slid quietly down from the clouds overhead, making its first noise when it hit the panes of the two windows of the wooden bungalow.

G was looking at a black-and-white reproduction of a painting hanging slightly above and to the right of a cupboard of unpainted wood. The reproduction was mounted and framed in a frame of varnished wood. The subject of the picture was a rural scene. Sheep grazed, hay stood in stooks, wheat ripened. In the foreground, a country lad, possibly a shepherd, wooed a girl. The girl looked at the country lad doubtfully. Flowers grew, apples lay by the girl's skirt.

'Well, those were the good old days when. . . . It's not the same today when you can't. . . . It strikes me. . . .'

As G sat looking at the picture, his mouth came slowly open. His gaze became unfocused.

Still the rain persisted. It ran slantingly down the panes; when G got up from where he was sitting in his wheel-back chair and gazed through the panes, they made a knotted visibility of the corner of the house that was available to his eyes.

He could see only one window on this side of the house. It was a small bow window with yellow or cream curtains, and it constituted the side or lesser window of a room which G knew to be Mr. Mary's bedroom, although he had never entered it.

Almost directly beneath the window, the corner of the house met the wall in which was set the brown side gate, forming an angle in which lay a dull and damp part of the garden. In the days when he had attempted to make something grow in this portion of the garden, G had been repeatedly unsuccessful. The stretch of lawn en-closed between the triangle composed of wall, house, and path grew less luxuriantly as it got nearer the house, so that it became as worn as a carpet from which all pile had been trodden by constant usage, although in fact nobody ever trod there. Against the wall of the house, the grass faded altogether, and was replaced by ferns. G could see the ferns now as he forced his gaze beyond the streaming windows. He knew they would be get-ting wet, but so strongly did the rain flow over the win-dow that he could gain no ocular corroboration of this.

With the rain came the darkness. Darkness fell early these January afternoons. Because the panes in the two windows of the wooden bungalow rested insecurely in their sockets, owing to the crumbling of the putty that surrounded them, and also because they had not been cut to make an exact fit to begin with, the rain soon began to trickle inside the sills. With the thickening of the light, it became impossible to see whether the rain came down on one or both sides of the panes.

Other features in the one room of the bungalow were also becoming submerged. On the calendar, the two men in period dress remained visible after the precipice below them had faded. The couch at the far end of the room failed to retain its shape in G's sight. The cupboard and the bamboo table merged into one ambiguous object. The paraffin lamp, burning with its transparent door split into four gleaming panels, assumed a new character entirely; the circular holes perforated in two sizes on its top cast a pattern of oval lights on the sloping roof overhead.

For a short while, as the room darkened into obscurity, it seemed by comparison that the two windows grew brighter and glowed with their own light; then they faded to become two patches in the dark, and the man was left to be in his own universe.

G was active; his right hand felt its way down the lapel and edge of his jacket until it reached the top button. The jacket was old. Its edge was ragged. The button too was ragged. It was made of leather. G remembered that it had once been sewn on by an uncle. He pushed it through the equivalent hole in the left side of his jacket. Then he rose from the chair, and felt for a galvanized bucket. Edging it forward, he pushed it into the corner

of the room under a stain that looked like a coral. He
returned to the wheelback chair.

After only the slightest interval, a clear metal noise
sounded in the dark. An identical noise followed almost
at once, and another, and another, and another, until a
point came in the sequence when G's idly attentive ear
could detect a change in the tones of the notes. They
continued by a very gradual degree to alter until the
metallic sound was lost altogether; in its place was a continuing liquid *plop,* as the bucket filled with rainwater.

On his seat G sat, his shoulder-blades pressed against
the four remaining supports, his legs stretched out before him, and his fingers curled under the seat of the
chair. The fingers of his left hand came in contact with
an irregularity on the underside of the chair seat; he
identified the irregularity as the date 1912, carved on the
chair when it was made. He rubbed his fingers back
and forth across the four digits.

'Are the fish glad to be caught?' he said quietly.

The rain continued steadily outside. A gust of wind
came, sending the water drops scattering. Some minutes
later, another gust came. Soon it was blowing steadily.
The outermost twigs of an elder tree which grew behind
the bungalow scraped across the back wall.

Even with the increased noise in the bungalow, the
drip of rain into the bucket was clearly audible. The
heaviness of the note finally reminded G that the bucket
was almost full. He got up, went over to it, felt for its
handle, straightened up with it and made his way carefully to the door. As he went, he heard the drips from
the roof fall to the floor.

He tugged at the door. It came quickly open and a

gust of wet air blew into his face. Descending onto the
one wooden step, he held the bucket by top and bottom,
swung it, and sent its contents flying out towards the
grass.

The bulk of the house was dark, except for a section
of it that included the small bow window of Mr. Mary's
bedroom. This section was lit by a street light that burned
on the other side of the brick wall in which stood the
brown side gate. This light threw the shadow of the wall
slantwise up the side of the house; it gleamed on the
bits of broken glass embedded in the wall and now
washed by the rain, casting their shadows also onto the
house.

G threw a look at the house and retreated into the
bungalow with the empty bucket. He slammed the door.
The door key fell out of the lock and dropped to the floor.

Without hurry, G took the bucket back to the corner
and stood it down there. The clear metallic noise began
again at once in the room.

Going over to the cupboard, G opened one of its doors
and felt inside for a candle and matches. He located
them, and stuck the candle, which was already partly
consumed, in the candlestick. He struck a match with
difficulty, hearing it grind too softly against the damp
side of the box, and then transferred its small flame to
the black twist of the candle's wick. When the candle
burned properly, he left it where it was and collected
the ingredients for a kettleful of tea. Into his small kettle
he put a handful of leaves of tea from a green packet,
adding to them a splash of milk from a tin of condensed
milk that bore two punched holes in its top. Taking up
a tin mug, he dipped it into the bucket filling it with

rainwater and poured this liquid into the kettle on top of the tea leaves and the condensed milk. He did this a second time, wiped the bottom of the kettle with a rag, and set it down on the paraffin stove. Then he blew out the candle, closed the cupboard, and returned to the wheelback chair, taking the tin mug with him.

Several sounds were distinguishable in the wooden room. The wind could be heard outside making several distinct noises in its course over different obstacles. The rain could be heard, making different vibrations, a light one on the window, a heavier drumming kind on the wooden sides of the bungalow, and a muffled kind on the asphalt of the roof overhead. The leak from the corner of the roof still contributed its noise into the bucket. The elder tree still raked the back of the bungalow with its twigs. To all these noises, another was later added. It was only a whisper of sound when G first detected it, but he had been anticipating it, and held it steadily in his attention until it grew stronger. Eventually it was loud. It cheered G.

To accompany the sound, a trickle of steam came from the spout of the kettle, which was deeply cleft, so that in the dim glow from the stove it looked like the open beak of a bird. The sound and the steam grew together in volume, the former now loud and insistent, the latter now a column that continued the line of the kettle spout outwards for some centimetres before billowing upwards in a cloud.

At first G gave no outward indication that he heeded these manifestations from his kettle. Only when the kettle lid became agitated by the pressure of steam inside, so that it jarred in its socket, did he stir. Removing the

33

kettle from the stove, he poured some of its contents into his tin mug. He set the kettle down by his right foot, where it would be handy for a refill.

The time taken to bring the kettle to a boil over a weak heat had been considerable. G was not in any hurry. It took him as long to drink the unsweetened contents of his mug. When he had drained the mug, he refilled it. By now the tea was cooling; he drank this second cup no faster than the first.

He rinsed out the mug in the bucket, which was now half full of water, and set it back in the cupboard beside the packet of tea and the tin of condensed milk. Then he freshened his hands and face in the bucket. Several drops of water fell from the roof into the hair on the crown of his head as he did so.

Picking up the bucket by the handle, he carried it over to the door and opened the door. Some wind and rain blew in upon him. He grasped the bucket with two hands and threw its contents clear of the steps. Then he came in and slammed the door as tightly as possible into its socket. Sometimes on windy nights, an extra strong gust would blow the door wide on its hinges.

After replacing the bucket in its corner, G walked to the other end of the room and sat down on the edge of the couch. He undid the laces of his boots and was easing them off his feet when a slight difference in the opacity of the gloom made him look up and out of the nearest window.

From where he sat on this side of the room, he could see through the streaming panes to the blank black west corner of the house and the blur of the garden beyond it. When he stood up and padded to the window, he could see the small bow window of that room he had never entered, the room that was Mr. Mary's bedroom. A light had just come on in the room. As G looked, a figure came to the window.

The figure was darkened by the light behind it. The street lamp faintly lit it, but the blur on the two panes of glass interposed in the space between G and the figure made all detail impossible to distinguish. The figure reached up its arms in a wide gesture and drew the curtains together across the bow window. A slight chink of light remained at the top of the curtains, then this was adjusted. There was no further sign from the window of the house. G waited where he was for some while.

'Another satisfied customer.'

He went back to his couch. He pulled off his trousers, set them carefully on the floor, and climbed on to the couch. Three blankets were lying on top of it. He worked his way under them, adjusted them round his stockinged feet, pillowed his head with one arm, and closed his eyes.

The bottom of the bucket was already covered by water leaking in from the roof, so that the metallic sound of dripping was replaced by the liquid sound of dripping. He lay listening to it for a certain passage of time.

When the bucket became full, the water started to pour down the sides of the bucket. It collected in a puddle about the bucket and commenced to trickle across the floor in a north-easterly direction. The wooden bungalow was built above the ground on ten low brick pillars which left a gap between the ground and the floor; some of these pillars had sunk slightly, so that the bungalow had a slight list towards the corner that stood nearest to the brick wall containing the brown side gate. This list was

35

sufficient to give the water a flow. It pushed outward until it touched the front wall of the bungalow, and then ran along beside that wall until it reached the gap under the door. The water then flowed away under the door and escaped into the soil beside the bungalow step.

'Several factors worth investigating there, when we get the instruments,' Midlakemela said briskly.

'The report is all very meticulous, but there's much it leaves out,' Domoladossa said. 'Temperatures, inside and outside, for instance.'

'And the boiling of G's kettle. Probability A is an entirely new continuum—we can take nothing for granted. The laws of our universe may not obtain there.'

'Quite. But what interests me is that the psychological make-ups of these people, G, Mary, and the rest may be alien to us. They may LOOK human, but they may not BE human.'

Midlakemela was less interested in that state of affairs. Instead, he glanced at his watches and said, 'Time for me to go to see the Governor. Anything you want?'

'No. I'll get on with the report.'

Midlakemela walked down the great curving room, treading the marked path among the bamboo screens. His superior officer sank back at his desk, absorbed in the report. He leaned forward, skipping the movements of G's life, until he reached a point on the morrow where G was emptying his bucket in the garden.

3

Because the concrete slabs were already partially dry after the night's rain, the thrown water left a clear ragged outline across them.

After G had observed this ragged outline, he stood gripping the empty bucket and looked to his right, across the garden. He saw the corner of the house round which the concrete path led; he saw the concrete path leading round the corner; he saw the various parts of the garden available to his vision, the privet hedges that in one place divided lawn from vegetable garden, that in another divided vegetable garden from fruit garden, that in another divided fruit garden from flower garden (though because the flower garden was in the main round the other side, the south-south-east side, of the house, it was rendered invisible to him by the bulk of the house), that in another divided the entire garden from the garden of another property owned by a man whose maternal grandfather had built a lighthouse in the southern hemisphere; he saw the asparagus bed that grew between the back of the house and the ancient brick coach house; he saw, perching on the roof of the ancient brick coach house, a homing pigeon whose name he had reason to suppose was X; he saw the tips of some of the fruit bushes, at present without leaf; he saw trees that would bear in their due season Victoria plums, Conference pears, and three sorts of apple: Cottenham Seedlings, Reinette du Canadas, and Court Pendu Plats; he saw the sundial, which was supported by an almost naked iron boy; he saw a linnet sitting on this sundial; he saw, by a slight further turn of his head towards the right, a line of beech trees that grew from the bottom and west corner of the garden parallel to the brick wall (that ran to join the street wall in which was the brown side gate) almost until they reached the point where the elder tree grew behind the wooden bungalow; he saw five varieties of birds sitting in the beech trees. Some of the birds sang. He saw no human beings in the garden.

When he swung his head quickly to the left again, he did not catch anyone looking at him from the window that belonged to Mr. Mary's bedroom.

Turning back, he deposited the empty bucket inside the door of the bungalow. He grasped the door by its metal doorknob. Exercising some force, he drew it shut. He walked forward until he got onto the concrete path at a point north of the ragged mark made by the water thrown from the bucket, and went to the side gate, which had been painted with a brown paint twenty-six months previously, when G had been in Mr. Mary's employ. G opened the gate and stepped into the road.

The road ran almost due north-west. It was wide and had pavements on both sides of it. Its surface was of a dark crumbly texture. On either side stood high brick walls, generally surmounted by embedded pieces of broken bottles, or railings painted green and ending in shapes like spears pointing to the sky; here and there were a private brewery, or shops at which tickets might be bought to enable one to travel to other towns in comfortable motor coaches, or large greenhouses shaped of glass and iron in which flowers and other things which had recently been growing might be bought; opposite the house was a café; at the far end of the road looking south-east were a cross of white marble and a group of lamp standards; there was also, behind the cross and the lamp standards, a low building with pillars along its front which was a railway station; from it came the sound of trains.

G waited beside a lamppost that stood on the pavement near the house and listened to the sound of trains. At the same time, he scanned the road to see if any cars were approaching from either direction. Because there were no cars, he crossed the road and went into the café.

Over the café ran a long board on which, in two sorts of letters, were printed the words 'Stationer Family G. F. WATT Grocer Café Snacks Draper.'

G. F. Watt struggled with a machine that made noises as it sucked dirt off the floor; he was too busy to move out of G's way. G squeezed between him and a large case that contained brightly coloured paper books and sat down at a small square table covered by a cloth printed with a design of red and white squares. G recognized the cloth. He put his hands on it as he sat down on a chair of wood constructed so that it could fold up into a small space when not in use. As G knew from a demonstration he had been given, the chair folded up efficiently, although it was not comfortable to sit on. G remembered he had once had an uncle who had sat on a chair which collapsed; G had not seen this happen, but the uncle had related the incident to him. The uncle had laughed when he related the incident.

Working methodically, G. F. Watt pushed the machine to the further end of the shop; there he switched it off and took it behind the counter, where he disappeared with it through a small door covered with an advertisement for a circus, leaving G alone in the café.

Through the café window, the front of the house could be seen; G surveyed it with care. The front door was reached by ascending two curved steps and was sheltered by a heavy stone porch, also curved, and supported by two stone pillars. To the left and the right of this door were windows. The window on the right—that is, the window nearest to the brown side gate—belonged to the sitting-room; the window to the left belonged to Mr. Mary's study. On the first floor were three windows; the one on the right, over the sitting-room, belonged to the room that was Mr. Mary's bedroom, as did the one in the middle over the front door, thus constituting the third window to this bedroom, the first one being the small bow window on the north-west side of the house visible from the wooden bungalow; the window on the left belonged to Mr. Mary's wife's bedroom. It had red curtains. Above these windows on the first floor, which were each of the same size and smaller than the two windows on the ground floor, was the line of the roof. The angles of the roof were capped by carved stone, as was the roof tree, which bore a weathered stone urn at each end. The roof was covered by blue-grey slates. In the middle of it was a small dormer window; this window belonged to the attic; projecting from the woodwork immediately above this small window was a white flagpole no more than a metre in length, which bore no flag. G had never seen it bear a flag.

To the left of the house, a section of red-brick garden wall had been removed to make room for a garage. This garage was constructed in a style and of materials different from those of the house. Large slabs of asbestos strengthened at intervals formed three of its sides, the front being entirely formed by two doors of a light metal. Small sealed windows were set above the doors at the front and in a similar position at the rear (the rear one being concealed from G's point of observation), the whole being capped by a corrugated metal roof.

Thus from G's post at the table in the café he could observe seven windows belonging to Mr. Mary's property; equally, he could be observed where he sat from seven windows belonging to Mr. Mary's property. He saw no movement at any of the windows.

G. F. Watt now returned through the door bearing the advertisement for a circus. He had disposed of the cleaning machine in the back regions of his premises; he bore a tray which he carried round the counter and placed on top of the red and white squared tablecloth, pronouncing as he did so a tentative opening to a conversation.

'Another strike in the car factory.'

'They say the conditions are bad.'

'Conditions have been worse.'

'I'm sure you are quite right, that is the price we have to pay for progress—conditions have always been worse. It's like in the fish shortages.'

'How do you mean? This is a fine piece of poached haddock.'

'In a fish shortage, the price of fish goes up.'

'Taste your poached haddock.'

'The coffee is good.'

'The haddock?'

'Excellent. Poached to a turn. Are you busy?'

'I haven't seen Mr. Mary's wife this morning.'

'Perhaps it's the strike?'

'How do you mean?'

'There's another strike in the car factory. They say conditions are bad.'

'How do you mean?'

'Men hanging about the streets. She might not like to go out.'

'I see what you mean.'

'Men hang about in the streets, you know.'

The two men both cast their gaze into the deserted road. G. F. Watt did not remove his until G had finished the meal; even then, he continued standing exactly where he was, close behind the chair that folded efficiently, so that when G rose to go he pushed the table forward to enable himself to rise. G moved to the door, opened it and went through onto the pavement. He looked up and down the road, found it empty of cars, and crossed it, heading for the brown side gate. The brown side gate was open, as he had left it.

G went through the gate and made for the wooden bungalow. When he reached it, he put his shoulder to the door of the wooden bungalow and pushed it open. The key lay inside on the floor, on the bare boards between the threshold of the door and the first of the fibre mats with green and orange stripes. G entered the bungalow without picking up the key.

Domoladossa thought, 'We'll have to decide. It may be possible to communicate with Probability A. We'll have to decide—I'll have to decide—whether these people have human responses.'

He glanced ahead at the report. He wanted to know about the rest of the occupants of the house. What did they do? What was their life about?

4

As G closed his door behind him, S walked round the west corner of the house, treading on the blocks of concrete that formed the path to the brown side gate and avoiding the cracks between the blocks. He reached the brown side gate, opened it, went through it, and shut it behind him.

For a while he stood on the edge of the pavement, breathing deeply and looking to his left and to his right. A car passed him, moving slowly with a flat tyre, and disappeared down the road towards the white marble cross. S crossed the road.

He entered the café opposite the house. Nobody was there. Inside the door to the left was a small table covered with a red-and-white squared cloth which S recognized;

44

there was a wooden chair beside the table, on which S sat; the seat of the wooden chair was not cold. S observed the house opposite. He noticed that the red curtain in one of the upper windows had not been drawn back tidily, so that it hung crookedly. He did not see anything move in any of the windows.

Behind the counter of the shop was a door covered by a poster advertising a circus that had once appeared locally; the circus had a Dozen Huge Untameable Lions performing in it. The door now opened. Through it came a man bearing a tray containing breakfast.

The man brought this tray round the counter and set the contents of the tray down upon the top of the table where S sat.

S looked down at a slice of haddock and adjusted it so that it lay in the middle of the white bone china plate. He spoke to the man who had brought the food.

'No doubt it is a lovely morning in Tahiti this morning.'

'How do you mean?'

'I said, No doubt it is a lovely morning in Tahiti today.'

'I see. Another strike at the car factory.'

'Fish looks nice.'

'Conditions are bad there, they tell me.'

'I compliment you on the taste also.'

'A fine piece of poached haddock.'

'Why are they striking?'

'They tell me conditions are bad there.'

'Higher wages, I suppose? Does she speak of it?'

'I haven't seen her this morning; she's afraid of men hanging about in the streets, so I hear.'

45

'What men? I don't see any.'

'How do you mean?'

'The street is empty.'

'It's early yet. Maybe about lunch time.'

'Mm, I see what you mean. Still, it is nice fresh fish.'

The man made no immediate reply to this, standing behind the folding chair on which S sat, resting his hands on the back of it, and gazing out at the road through his shop window.

S also gazed out of the shop window as he sat eating. He gazed across the road at the house.

Because the house was directly opposite, only the front of it could be observed from the café. It presented a symmetrical picture, with the window to the left of the front door being balanced by the window to the right of the front door. The door itself was painted with a glossy green paint and had a crescent-shaped fanlight over it; it was reached by two curved steps and sheltered by a heavy stone porch, also curved, and supported by two stone pillars.

On the first floor there were three windows overlooking the street, the middle one being placed over the front door; and above this middle window was a small dormer window set in the roof with a small flagstaff protruding above it. The flagstaff bore no flag.

The dormer window, S knew, belonged to an attic room. Of the three windows below, the one on the left belonged to Mr. Mary's wife's bedroom, while the other two belonged to Mr. Mary's bedroom. On the ground floor, the window to the left of the front door belonged to Mr. Mary's study; the one on the right belonged to the sitting-room.

In none of these windows was there any movement. 'Not much doing over there this morning.'

To the south-east of the house, facing onto the road, was a garage, separated from the house only by a couple of metres. Although obviously built at a more recent date than the house, it presented some of the aspects of shabbiness. It was constructed of slabs of asbestos and pillars of reinforced concrete, apparently of a prefabricated pattern. Two double doors of a light metal occupied all the front wall of the garage. Above these doors, set under the peak of the roof, was a small square sealed window, its area of glass divided into four by a pair of crossed bars; from one of these small squares, the glass was missing. There was no movement visible through the small sealed window. The garage was covered by a corrugated metal roof.

'I hear that in a fish shortage the price of fish goes up.'

'People aren't as honest as they used to be. But I enjoyed the haddock.'

'Nice piece of poached haddock, that.'

S pushed the small table forward so that he could get up. He walked round a large case that contained brightly coloured paper books, opened the door, and walked out onto the pavement. A man was hurrying along the pavement wearing a woollen scarf about his neck and carrying a bicycle over his left shoulder; the bicycle had a green hooter and two flat tyres. He did not speak to S. S waited till he had disappeared and then crossed the road, heading for the brown side gate. He opened it and walked in.

Shutting the gate behind him, he drew the bolt into

position and commenced to walk along the concrete path, taking care not to tread on the cracks between the concrete blocks. On his left hand was the house, to which he drew nearer as the path led him towards its west corner. On his right was a wooden bungalow; he regarded it from the corner of his right eye, and observed a small movement through the window to the left of the door. As he directed his gaze straight ahead again, his vision took in the image of a black and white cat bounding away from him in a westerly direction, running past a sundial supported by an iron boy. The cat darted through a gap in a privet fence dividing grass from vegetable garden, and was hidden among cabbages. A pigeon sometimes referred to as X rose heavily from the other side of the cabbage patch, circled cumbrously twice, and flew with a clatter of wings towards the old brick building behind the house.

S stepped over a ragged damp patch that spread over the path and continued straight until he reached the west corner of the house, turning it without pause, though at a slower rate.

In the middle of the rear or south-west face of the house was set the back door; at this door the concrete path terminated. S pursued it to within two metres of this terminal point and then turned right, along a path that had been worn in a stretch of grass. The path was muddy from the night's rain. A sparrow which sat upon it flew off it and perched on a privet hedge as S approached. The path led to a gravel walk heading directly away from the house, and along this S walked. He now had the back of the house directly at his back; on his right hand was a privet hedge that bordered the walk;

on his left hand lay three long mounds with furrows
between them; these were the asparagus beds; under-
foot was the gravel walk, in which, because the gravel
was sparse and much trodden in to the earth, small weeds
such as groundsel grew, bearing little flowers even at
this time of year.

Both furrows and gravel walk led to a two-storey brick
building. The brick had turned to a gentle orange with
age; much of it was concealed by ivy which grew in
several places from the ground up to the guttering. In
the front of the building, old grey timbers ran among
the brick. The lower half of this façade was mainly timber, and consisted of two heavy doors, the hinges of which
had collapsed, letting the bottoms of the doors sink into
the gravelly earth. In the upper halves of these doors
were the frameworks for a double row of square panes
of windows, but most of the panes had been broken and
replaced by sheets of wood or cardboard or pieces of
sacking; even the panes that remained were curtained
by the cobwebs of many generations of spiders. The wood
of these doors had attained a texture like elephant hide
where weather had wrinkled and pitted it.

Above the old doors, the brickwork began again and
continued up to the eaves, interrupted only by a round
and dusty window divided into nine panes, the central
one of which was square. At the peak of the brickwork,
under the V of the roof, a pattern of eight holes was
set, their bases streaked with dirt. In one of these holes
sat a homing pigeon called X; when it saw S approaching,
it fluttered upwards with heavy strokes of its wings and
landed on the tiling of the roof.

In one of the old doors, the right hand one, was a

smaller door, no more than one and an half metres high. Having reached the old brick building, S put his hand to the catch of this small door and pushed it open. Before entering the aperture, he paused and glanced over his shoulder.

The back of the house was some thirty-five metres away; it stood on a slightly higher level than did the old brick building, for the gravel walk leading to the latter had sloped down a dip in the ground. From this elevation, five windows were visible, excluding the small pane of bottle glass in the centre of the back door. One of these windows was open; this was the downstairs window on the left of the back door; it was the kitchen window, and through it the head of Mr. Mary's wife could be discerned bowed over some business at the sink.

Showing signs of hurry, S bent his back and entered the brick building through the small aperture, pulling the door closed after him and securing it on the inside by a loop of cord attached to the door, which he draped over a nail knocked part way into the ancient timber of the larger door in which the small one was set.

As he read, Domoladossa felt a sense of privilege. A week ago, he and all his millions of fellow men were living in a world of apparent uni-probability. Then this other continuum manifested itself. Who knew, there could be a myriad different probability worlds? But he was one of the first to read the report on Probability A.

He experienced danger as he read. This house, and the outhouse S was entering—they were so banal that you'd never look at them twice in ordinary life. But did

*Probability A contain ordinary life? Were the very mol-
ecules of the bricks different? Or would the fact of their
all being the same make the whole business even more
miraculous?*

*And this was just Probability A. A myriad probabilities.
. . . The Gods had been not merely prodigal but mad.*

*A photograph of his wife stood on Domoladossa's desk.
He gazed at it tenderly. There would be continua where
they had never met, of course . . . Then he returned to
the report.*

The inside of the old brick building was large enough
to house a private carriage such as prosperous people
drove in the days before automobiles were invented. The
floor space was partly filled by a bench along the right-
hand wall; several old oil drums that stood along the
rear wall; a motor-driven lawn mower and a miscellany
of garden tools that stood or leaned along the left-hand
wall; and a number of boxes, broken pieces of furniture,
a tin trunk with the initials H.S.M. stencilled large upon
it, a rusty bird cage, a garden roller, a kitchen mangle
with a bicycle leaning against it with flat tyres, a pile
of sacks, a petrol can, several lengths of copper piping,
and various other oddments, all lying about the floor,

chiefly at the rear or south-west end of the brick building.

Also at that end of the building was a solid wooden structure of steps leading up to the room above. S advanced to this structure and ascended the steps, placing his feet with care as well as speed, for the treads had been unevenly hollowed in the middle.

As he ascended, his head, and consequently his eyes, came level with and then rose above the floor of the upper room, a rough, splintery, and uneven floor of old planks which was streaked here and there in no particular pattern with areas of smoothness—round a knot in the wood, or along the side of a board raised slightly higher than its neighbours; these smooth parts were of a lighter yellow tone than the predominant rough areas of wood.

Walking indiscriminately over these areas, S proceeded to the front of the room in eight and a half paces, stopped, and knelt. He could now see out of the round window that was divided into nine sections. Gazing through one of these sections, S stretched out his right hand to a point where the brickwork to the right of the round window curled into a small niche; putting his hand into the niche, S brought out a telescope.

This instrument was familiar to him. He had bought it about fifteen months ago, before Mr. Mary had dismissed him, from an antique dealer whose nose was peppered with small white pimples no bigger than freckles. When closed, the telescope measured some fifteen centimetres in length, it was bound in worn leather. S pulled one end of it, revealing three brass tubes which extended out of each other. On the barrel of the smallest tube, the legend 22X was engraved, signifying that the telescope was capable of magnifying objects glimpsed through it twenty-two times. At the top of the smallest tube was the eyepiece, which S now raised to his right eye. Directing the telescope to point towards the house, he closed his left eye and stared with the other through the barrel of the telescope.

He was now viewing the world through five thicknesses of glass, four consisting of the lenses in his telescope and one of the small square panels of glass that formed the centre of the nine glass segments together comprising the round window. These layers of glass lent their slight coloration to the view.

The little circle of his vision was surrounded by black. He could not examine much of the view at one time.

He extended the telescope further. A red mist swam before his staring eye. He closed the telescope slightly. The red mist acquired texture and horizontal and vertical markings. S's circle of vision slid over the rear wall of the house; it descended; it hovered for a moment on the back door and discerned the pane of green bottle glass that served the back door as a small window; and then it moved to the left, seeing brickwork again before it alighted on the kitchen window.

This window was different from the others of the house. The other windows were wooden framed; this was a window with metal frames. The metal frame was longer than it was high and supported three sub-sections, each of which carried six panes of glass; of these three sub-sections, the middle one was a fixture, but the two on either side of it opened, and had perforated metal bars to secure them when they were open. The window on the right was open at the present, and secured on the third perforation of its metal bar.

The circle of S's vision slid over the window, came back, and settled on its target. The blackness now eclipsed everything but a tiny portion of brickwork, a sliver of metal frame, part of the open window viewed obliquely because it projected towards the watcher, and the small section of the kitchen framed within this opening.

Within the small section of the kitchen framed in the opening, a proportion of the figure of Mr. Mary's wife was visible. Tinted slightly by the layer of glass interposed between her and the watcher's eye, she exposed to view, covered by a blue cardigan, something more than half her body from a line drawn by the window sill about ten centimetres above her waist: of her trunk, her left breast and shoulder were clearly visible, covered by the blue cardigan, which in turn was partially covered by an apron, two strings of which ran over the shoulders; possibly because this apron had faded, or because its pattern was small and confused, its colour registered only as a blur through the telescope.

The woman's left arm was visible; it moved to and fro, and could be seen lifting articles out of a sink. Sometimes the right arm became visible during this process, and then frequently more of her body would become visible, her right breast and right shoulder, sometimes including her right elbow. The sleeves of the blue cardigan were rolled up to a point above the elbows, so that the flesh of her arms below the elbow was visible. Viewed through the layers of glass interposed between it and the watcher's eye, the arms were of a greyish pink.

55

The face of the woman could not be examined very satisfactorily through the telescope because she stood with her gaze bent downwards, directed at the objects with which she dealt in the sink. But since she occasionally glanced upwards, quizzing to her left and right, and on three occasions looked behind her to ascertain if anyone was standing there, and once stared vacantly into the garden, allowing her hands to be idle at the same time, it was possible to obtain a sort of symposium view of her whole head and all the features on it. Although her hair was not tidily arranged, it had a parting in the centre of the skull; how far back this parting went could not be distinguished, since the hair that grew at the back of the skull had been brushed upwards and secured by small metal clips to the hair on the crown of the skull. Some locks of hair had escaped this confinement; over the right shoulder hung a strand that trailed down until it touched the string of the apron, while on the left side of the woman's face, several wisps of hair bobbed over the temple or, curling behind the ear, rose up from underneath the lobe and touched the left cheek. On the crown of the skull, the hair seemed a middle brown in tone, but the ends of it, and in particular the lock that trailed on the right shoulder, were more golden, so that the whole effect was of a tawniness. The eyebrows were darker, and straight rather than curved. They were long and ample. Below the eyebrows were set two eyes with heavy lids. Viewed from a distance, even under twenty-two orders of magnification, the colour of the iris was difficult to distinguish; they appeared sometimes to have the same shade of tawniness as the hair; at other moments they seemed more hazel.

These pupils were slow in movement, and often seemed scarcely visible under the eyelids. Between the eyes, the bridge of the nose was hardly distinguishable at this distance, because it was not high; the nose only rose to any prominence at its lower extremity, where it swelled out into a small bulb set with wide nostril flanges on either side, giving a total effect of a nose of some degree of good nature, weakness, and impertinence. Below this again was the upper lip and then the mouth, pale and unpainted, with an ample lower lip that protruded slightly; the corners of the mouth were tucked firmly into the cheeks. The chin was rounded and firm, youthful, and with resolution in its lines when it was tucked into the neck, as it was when the face was directed downwards. The cheekbones were fairly high and set wide apart. The skin covering them was fresh and a more delicate shade of pink than the arms, as far as could be determined through the telescope.

Although the effect of this face might have been interpreted by an onlooker as generally indolent, it was continually in movement, so much so as sometimes to elude the small circle of telescopic vision which sought to keep it always in the centre of its focus. The eyes under their heavy lids sometimes looked this way and sometimes that at the objects being given attention in the sink or being brought out of the sink and placed on a shelf or ledge next to it; also the head moved, not only from one side to the other, but—on one occasion— tilted upwards as the woman gazed vaguely into the garden beyond the window, her attention possibly being distracted (without being definitely attracted) by a brief flight made by a pigeon from the peak of the roof of the old brick building into an apple tree; and on three occasions the woman turned her body slightly and head entirely to see if someone was behind her in the kitchen. The woman's hands were more continuously in motion, being involved with the objects in the sink, which they repetitively brought out of the sink, placing them on a shelf or ledge next to it. On one occasion, one of the hands, the left one, rose up to the left cheek, which lowered itself slightly to meet the hand, in order to brush back a curl of the hair that had escaped from the confinement of metal clips on the crown of the skull.

When all the objects had been removed from the sink, the woman stepped away from it, turning and moving towards the rear of the kitchen, where an impoverishment of light made her difficult to see through the telescope.

When S removed the telescope from his eye, she became only a vague movement in the lower left-hand window of the house set on a slight rise in the ground beyond the asparagus beds. He blinked, rubbed his closed eye on his sleeve, and then reapplied the instrument to the pupil of his right eye.

Now the circle of his vision moved restlessly to and fro across the kitchen window with its metal frame, the left third of which opened outwards and was secured by a perforated metal bar, as it sought to follow the movements of the woman in the kitchen.

The woman was far enough into the room to be encompassed by its shadows; what she was doing could not be distinguished. But she moved slowly behind a table, thus coming to be viewed through the middle and unopening portion of the kitchen window that was divided into six panes. S was now gazing at her through

six thicknesses of glass, four of them being in the telescope, one being the square central pane of the nine small
panes that together comprised the round window in the
old brick building, which had last housed a coach forty-
eight years before Mr. Mary had purchased the property,
and the final one being the unopening middle portion
of the kitchen window. The woman moved to the near
side of the kitchen table, coming close enough to the
window for her to be revealed using a white towel. This
white towel was held at breast level; it was in constant
motion as the woman's two hands rubbed themselves dry
in it. The woman, continuing her progress, moved over to
the section of the window which remained closed, and
leant her elbows on a ledge or shelf that stretched to this
side of the sink as it did to the other; although her hands
were still engaged in drying themselves on the towel,
this new posture enabled the woman to lean forwards
from the waist up; the weight of her breasts could vaguely
be seen, indicated by the swell of the apron which she
wore over her blue cardigan, and which she had not removed. In thus leaning forward, the woman brought her
face within a few centimetres of the closed window, so
that it was clearly revealed in the light.

As the face was tilted slightly upwards, so the nose
became somewhat the predominant feature; it was a button nose with nostril flanges that spread slightly in the
direction of either cheek. It could be seen to have a
slight pinkness that almost exactly matched the colour in
the cheeks; the cheek bones were relatively high, and set
wide apart, giving the whole face width. The face tapered
towards a smoothly rounded chin that at present seemed
to protrude because of the stance the woman adopted.

59

The woman rested her elbows on a ledge or shelf that extended to the side of the sink. She clasped in her hands a white towel that partially concealed her face, in particular her right cheek; the irregular shape of the towel contrasted with the smooth sweep of her visible left cheek. The high bones of this cheek, concealed but evident, gave to her eyes the effect of being set rather deeply in her face; this effect was emphasized by the heaviness of the eyelids that covered the eyes. These features might be regarded as belonging to a fleshy face; yet the effect was not heavy when the face was in movement.

At present the face was in movement; it lay within the circle of vision of the telescope with its mouth at the centre of this circle.

The mouth moved. The lips moved; the lower lip seemed to be plump, yet as it moved it extended itself slightly so as to seem less plump. These lips were viewed through six thicknesses of glass, four consisting of the little lenses in the telescope, one consisting of the square of glass that formed the central panel of the nine glass panels together comprising the round window in the front of the old brick building, and one consisting of the openable but closed portion of the kitchen window. So near was this closed portion of the kitchen window to the moving lips that the breath issuing between them had fogged the pane, obscuring still further both the right cheek already obscured by the towel and a part of the towel itself. The straining right eye that watched through the telescope could just discern a tongue in movement, and the tips of white teeth revealed by the lower lip when the mouth opened widely.

Accompanying this activity of the mouth, the head also

moved, chiefly with a sort of nodding that kept time with the lip movements. The hair untidily nodded. In the front, this hair had been neatly parted in the middle, and then swept back; evidently it was gathered together by some device at the rear of the skull; the loose ends had then been bunched carelessly (or hastily) forward and secured against the crown of the skull on top of the neat hair by small metal clips; this hair nodded now like a wave breaking. It was tawny hair, rather dark over the crown, more of a golden tone at the ends. Against the right side of the woman's neck was a thick tawny lock; this was swinging with the movement of the head. The eyes were wider open than formerly, so that less of the heavy lids was on display; the irises appeared to be perhaps of a thick golden colour.

Domoladossa pencilled a note in the margin of the report: 'She was singing.'

He wanted to add, 'She was happy,' but that would be carrying the job of interpretation too far.

He was almost breathless with the thought of the happiness of this alien woman, a happiness that the impartiality of the report seemed to heighten. He considered the passage he had just read extremely erotic, and wondered how the Governor would take it.

Eagerly, he read on.

The woman turned from the window with a quick movement. She moved across the kitchen, keeping parallel with the sink. She held her head high, so that its details

were lost in the poor light, but it appeared that her
mouth was still opening and closing by the movement of
the muscles in her neck and the bobbing of her chin,
though these details too were uncertain since the woman
was progressing erratically, taking certain rhythmic steps
that made her shoulders rise and sink. At the same time,
she spread her arms to shoulder height and waved them
while keeping them level; in her right hand she still re-
tained the white towel. She rotated once through three
hundred and sixty degrees in a clockwise direction, wav-
ing her hands as she did this. When she was again
proceeding across the kitchen in her previously determined direction parallel with the sink, she crossed behind
the third of the window that was open and disappeared
from sight.

S lowered the telescope. He looked through the dusty
window that was divided into nine sections, several of
them draped with small webs from which spiders had
gone, and stared at the house some thirty-five metres
away. He could see the lower left-hand window that
belonged to the kitchen with its right-hand section open.
He blinked his eyes and nipped the bridge of his nose
with the thumb and index finger of the left hand. He saw
a movement in the kitchen.

Lifting the telescope to his right eye, S closed his left
eye. He held the instrument near to the eyepiece with his
right hand, gripping it with his left hand at the other
extremity, where the barrel was bound in leather; doing
this necessitated bending both elbows; he rested the left
elbow on the lower extremity of the brick ledge that
surrounded the round window. Even with this support,
the circle of vision trembled slightly as it moved with its

encompassing darkness over the asparagus bed, not fo-
cusing on the earth, and up across a confused patch of
lavender and shrub and path and grass, and swam up the
brickwork with its pattern of horizontal and vertical lines,
until it settled on the open third of the kitchen window.

The woman was dimly visible, standing away from the
window with her back to it. She had rid herself of the
white towel. Her hands were behind her back, and consequently visible to the spectator. They appeared more
pink at the extremities than were the arms. The hands
were busy with the strings of the apron; they undid them,
dropped the strings, and moved up to the woman's
shoulders; there they took hold of the apron string that
ran behind the woman's neck, lifted it over the woman's
head, and carried the apron by it out of sight.

The circle of vision lingered over the open portion of
window. All that could clearly be seen through the open
window was a corner of a table; shadows lay behind the
table. The circle trembled. Once it moved away from the
window, travelled towards the right, inspected the back
door with its square pane of green bottle glass, moved
right again, looked into the window of the room on the
right of the back door, which was the dining-room, slid
upwards over the pattern of the brickwork with its horizontal and vertical lines, and then worked left again,
peering over the sills of the three windows on the first
floor as it went: the window of the bathroom, the central
window, belonging to a spare bedroom, and another window belonging to a second spare bedroom; in all of
these windows, no movement could be sighted. The
circle of vision slanted away across the house as S removed the telescope from his eye.

He blinked and pinched his nose at the bridge with the index finger and thumb of his left hand. Using both hands, he pressed both ends of the telescope so that the three brass sections slid one into the other and all slid into the outer barrel, which measured some fifteen centimetres; it was bound in worn leather.

6

S stood upright, put his hands into his pockets, removed them almost at once, brushed the knees of his trousers, and returned his hands to the pockets. He yawned and blinked his eyes.

The floor of the room was built of thick wooden planks running from side to side in which two colours predominated, a darker brown tone in the hollows, where the timber was rough and splintery, and yellow on the raised parts, which had been smoothed by tread; the effect was approximately of tawny hair. S crossed the length of this flooring in ten paces until he stood by the top of the rough hewn structure of wooden steps that led up from the floor below.

A square trapdoor also made of wood leant against the

back wall of the room. S grasped it with his right hand and brought it over, first pulling and then lowering it, until the trapdoor fitted into a groove and the structure of wooden steps was concealed from view.

Near to the spot where the trapdoor had rested when it was open was a small square window, hardly bigger than a man's hand and situated only half a metre above the floor. This small window occupied the centre of the back wall of the room. Although its glass was cracked and dirty, a view could be seen through it if one stooped down. It looked out across a small patch of ground filled by straggling elder bush and nettles to the privet hedge dividing the garden from a garden beyond it. Of the four sides of the square plot of land belonging to Mr. Mary, this boundary behind the old brick building was the only one not marked by a brick wall. The privet hedge was a metre and a quarter high. On the other side of it lay the property of a single man whose maternal grandfather had constructed a lighthouse in the southern hemisphere; it was said that this architectural achievement had been acknowledged by a knighthood. S glanced out of the small square window and then straightened his back. He began to walk up and down the room.

It was only possible to walk upright near the central axis of the room. Overhead sloped the bare beams that supported the roof of the old brick building; the curling orange tiles were visible between the beams, with chinks of light among them where they had become dislodged. Along the two long sides of the room, the roof sloped down to within a metre and a half of the floor. These side walls and the front and rear walls had at some date been whitewashed; at a later date, they had been papered with wallpaper of a light orange colour covered with bunches of flowers as big as dinner plates, each bunch divided from the next by a representation of brown trellis. Much of this paper had peeled away or had been pulled off. In the blank spaces where it had hung, the bricks showed through the old whitewash. When the whitewash was touched, it came off in a cloud of powder.

The rear or south-west wall of the room rose up to a central point to meet the long central roof tree. The corresponding central point on the front or north-east wall of the room was not visible, for, at a short distance below, a platform had been built out into the room. This platform was the floor of a small compartment designed for pigeons and entered from without by a pattern of eight holes let into the brickwork for that purpose. Only one pigeon, designated X, now used this pigeon loft, the rear of which was boarded across so that birds could not enter the attic.

The long central roof tree was supported in three places by beams and cross-beams, the latter coming down to within a metre and a half of the tawny floor. As he walked up and down, S avoided these three low cross-beams in a practised manner, ducking his head and shoulders without breaking his stride or removing his hands from the pockets of his trousers.

Near the middle one of these three cross-beams, and placed to one side so that its lid almost touched the tiles, was a black stove. The stove stood on an iron tray. Although cylindrical in shape, from top to bottom the stove was embellished by grills, traps, doors, lids, vents, slides, dampers, patent pokers, spinwheels, knobs, sliding panels, catches, bulges, decorations, flanges, and a mica eye no larger than the eyepiece of S's telescope. The lid on top was ornamented, while round the lid on the body of the stove, written there in florid and raised imitation of a person's handwriting, were the words Stentorian 1888. These two words almost surrounded the lid.

From a point at the back of the stove rose a pipe thicker than a man's upper arm. The upper end of it, which was protected from rain by a raised and jointed cap, protruded through the roof, thus enabling any smoke generated in the stove to be released outside.

Beside the stove, in the iron tray on which the stove stood, lay pieces of wood of various kinds, pithy lengths of elder wood, beech twigs, a stout piece of bamboo, broken and hairy strips of white wood off some kind of packing case—one or two with nails protruding from them—and dark fragments of wood that might have been chopped off old furniture. A hatchet lay beside the wood.

When S had walked up and down the room past the stove some two dozen times, thus avoiding the three low beams some six dozen times, and each time without pausing in his stride or removing his hands from the pockets of his flannel trousers, he retired to a log of wood close by the round window that gave a view of the back of the house, and sat down upon it. This log bore on its uppermost surface innumerable scars where it had been struck by a blade, possibly by a hatchet. Most of the cuts were less than five centimetres long. Where two or more intersected, the bark of the log had in some cases sprung away, revealing a triangle of the lighter wood underneath.

Apart from the log and the stove, the room contained only two pieces of furniture.

One of these pieces was hung between the first and the second of the low cross-beams. It was a canvas hammock. From each end of this hammock, a converging series of ropes ran to a pair of thick metal rings; these rings were hung over two large nails driven deep, one into the first and one into the second of the beams. From the hammock hung the corners of two grey blankets and an arrangement of sacks stuffed with folded newspaper and strung together with garden twine to form a kind of bedspread.

The other piece of furniture was a long arrangement of shelves and partitions which stood along the southeast wall, on S's left hand as he sat on the log with his back to the round window that commanded a view of the house. This shelving had once been used to house various equipment appertaining to pigeons, nesting boxes, bags filled with round black pellets, perches, grit, small numbered rings made of a metal like pewter.

Some of this equipment still remained, though in the main the shelving was monopolized by articles belonging to or acquired by S.

Among these articles, the following could be distinguished: a storm lantern of antique design; a bowler hat; two empty jam jars; a patent inhaler made to fit the nostril; a streamlined pottery representation of a carthorse, the head missing; a pair of nail clippers; a collection of nail clippings, gathered in an ash tray; a mousetrap; part of the skeleton of a long-eared bat, discovered during an expedition to the chamber below; a brief-case purchased on the day that S had been given the post of secretary to Mr. Mary; the leg of an upright chair, worm-eaten; a fountain pen constructed of a tartan plastic; a hot water bottle; a brass handle off a drawer; a cotton reel on which was wound brown thread, with a needle balanced on the top of it; a pigskin purse, lying open and empty; a chipped china candlestick on which had been printed a crude representation of the devil; a paperbound book with a curled-up cover entitled 'The Penguin Handyman'; three walnuts; a coach lantern with its glass smashed; another empty jam jar; an umbrella, across which lay a straw hat with a red and blue band round it; an oval notice made of metal coated with enamel, on which was printed the legend Beware of the Dog; an oblong notice of the same materials bearing the same legend; a punched bus ticket; a comb with teeth missing; a hair brush with hair missing; an upright shaving mirror with the mirror missing; an elaborate iron key; a cigarette packet; a free luncheon voucher; another jam jar, this one containing purple runner bean seeds; a brass hinge; an oily rag; a small basin with a floral design containing a razor, a shaving brush, and a spoon; a rag; a slice of green soap; an enamel chamber pot without handle; a brass crocodile eight centimetres long; a small collection of groceries and eating utensils, among which a blue and white striped cup and a packet of tea were noticeable; a row of books, including a 'Typist's Desk Book'; 'Low Point X'; Victor Hugo's 'Les Misérables'; 'Pickwick Papers' without its cover; 'Pregnancy—Conception to Childbirth'; Band I of Spengler's 'Der Untergang des Abendlandes'; 'Toys Through the Ages'; 'Living for Jesus'; 'First Steps in the Bible'; 'First Steps in Chemistry'; 'First Steps in Philosophy'; 'Understanding God'; 'A Shorter Shorthand Manual'; 'Sex in Practice'; 'Black's Picturesque Tourist of England'; 'My Alps', by Mrs. Meade; and the 'Boy's Own Paper' for the second week in August, 19—.

None of these articles was free of dust. The dust was like a very fine powder, and sometimes noticeably white or orange in tone.

S selected the 'Boy's Own Paper' and sat down on the scarred log with it. He began to read episode three of The Secret of The Grey Mill. When he had read the first two columns, he put the magazine down, laying it on the planking open and face-upwards, and knelt to look out of the round window.

S, the watchful S, the ex-secretary—there was something predatory about him. A more menacing character than G, thought Domoladossa. But could events so be interpreted? Suppose this strange world, this Probability A, was so strange it knew no sin? Suppose God had a myriad worlds, all lying there like nursery beds, in which He tried out various combinations of sin or innocence?

As he conjectured, Domoladossa's eyes rested on the desk photograph of his wife. From beyond its convenient frame, the Distinguishers were watching him.

There were four Distinguishers on duty at present, all standing gravely in the open air, gazing at the tall manifestation, on which Domoladossa could be seen at his desk, leafing through the report.

'He looks much as we do.'

'Obviously a world of almost co-determinate synchronicity.'

'But we have no key to scale.'

'Scale?'

'*He may be no bigger than my thumb. He may be as tall as a house.*'

'*Keep watching. His entire probability-sphere may evaporate at any minute, like a puff of steam.*'

Part Two

S The Watchful

1

The Distinguishers stood on their hillside, solemnly staring at the curious mirage in the air, on which was a representation of a world to which they had only just discovered limited access.

The screen depicted a man called Domoladossa, who was leaning comfortably back in a chair, doing nothing but read a report. Domoladossa was as occupied by his report as the Distinguishers were with him. The affairs of his life were forgotten while he followed the activities of an unknown man called S, who saw fit to examine the back door of a house through his telescope.

Below the door was a stone step. This stone step had two features, one permanent, one temporary. The permanent feature stood on the right, the temporary feature stood on the left. The permanent feature was a shoe scraper of ornamental ironwork, the two ends of which curved upwards like dragons' heads; through the telescope's circle of vision, it was impossible to determine if they were intended to represent dragons' heads. At the other end of the step stood a milk bottle. It was empty, and had been washed, so that the brickwork of the house was visible through it, though dulled and distorted. As S inspected the milk bottle through the telescope, a slight wash of colour and light spread over the bottle and over the step, so that the bottle took on a gleam along its sloping shoulders. At the same time, a dead leaf whisked through the circle of vision, over the step, and was gone into the darkness that always surrounded the circle of vision.

Lowering the telescope, S blinked his eyes and looked out of the round window. Pale sunshine lay across the garden. It came through the round window at an oblique angle and touched a little of the woodwork and an even smaller strip of the brick to the lower left-hand side of the window. If S had leant forward and looked past the south corner of the house in a south-easterly direction, he would have seen the sun appearing through cloud. Instead, he returned the telescope to his right eye and directed it towards the house.

The empty milk bottle stood on the left of the stone step below the back door. It floated in the centre of the circle of vision. The centre of vision moved up to the knob of the door; it moved left over the brickwork to peer in through the open kitchen window; it moved right to peer in through the dining-room window; it moved upwards to peer in through the bathroom window; it slid left again to peer in through the two windows of the two spare rooms; it returned to the doorstep, over which a shadow now fell as a cloud moved across the sun; this cloud movement was the only movement it detected on its tour.

Gradually the circle of vision moved away from the house. It slid to the right. It picked out the back of the garage built of asbestos and concrete. There was a door in the back of the garage. Above the door, under the peak of the garage roof, was a small square window divided into four square panes; one of the four panes was missing. The telescope was not focused to pick out the details of the garage clearly.

Sliding away from the garage, still moving towards the right, the circle of vision picked out the brick wall that ran from behind the garage to mark the south-east boundary of the property. Above this wall, some distance on the other side of it, rose the steeple of a church; the telescope was not focused to reveal the steeple properly; it remained blurry; prismatic colours ran up and down it, particularly down its left side.

S removed the telescope from his eyes. He yawned and blinked. With the thumb and index finger of his left hand, he pinched the bridge of his nose. He changed the telescope into his left hand and rubbed his forehead and eyes with his right hand. He returned the telescope to his right hand and applied the eyepiece to his eye; simultaneously, he steadied the far end of the telescope with his left hand and directed the instrument towards the house.

The circle of vision came to rest on the guttering that

ran along the roof. At either end of the roof, the guttering met vertical drainpipes before continuing round the angles of the house to serve the rest of the roof. The circle of vision slid down the left of these two vertical drainpipes, and slid across the two windows of the two spare bedrooms, moving slowly so as not to miss any movement within the room, but moving continuously. When it reached the next window along, the window of the bathroom, it paused. All that could be distinguished through the bathroom window was a lamp-shade with a short length of flex above it, pointing upwards to the ceiling before being obscured by the upper casement of the window; the shade was so obscured by shadow that its colour could not be made out through the telescope. There was no movement in the bathroom.

Slipping downwards, the circle of vision inspected the long windows of the dining-room; no movement could be detected behind them. The circle of vision moved to the back door, noted that the empty milk bottle still stood on the left of the step, and moved on to the window of the kitchen. The right-hand portion of this window was open to admit air to the room; through the aperture could be distinguished the top of a table; on the top of the table, but half hidden from the watcher's view by one of the uprights of the window, was an object that resembled a basket. There was no movement in the kitchen.

Bringing the telescope away from his right eye, S laid it on the flooring below the round window. He did not press its four sections together. He rubbed both hands over his eyes. He peered at the house through the square centre panel of glass of the round window.

He could just see the milk bottle standing on the step

below the back door. He could not see the shape that
resembled a basket inside the kitchen. He could not see
any movement in any of the windows of the house. He
picked up 'The Boy's Own Paper' for the second week of
August 19—, and took it over to the log with the numer-
ous cuts on its upper surface. He sat down on the log and
began to read the third episode of a serial entitled The
Secret of the Grey Mill, commencing from a sentence at
the bottom of the second column: Clutching Tom's arm,
Frank Masters pointed towards the open door.

When S had read to the bottom of the next page, he
reached a sentence which said, Thirsty though he was, he
watched the brackish water drain away without regret.
At this point, S stopped reading and put the magazine
down on the flooring, open and face upwards. With the
thumbnail of his right hand, he picked between two front
teeth in his lower jaw. As he did this, he looked about
him.

Along the two long sides of the room, the roof with
its curling orange tiles sloped down to within about a
metre and a half of the floor. For the most part, these side
walls and the two end walls were papered with wallpaper
of a light orange; this paper had a pattern of large bunches
of flowers divided from each other by a sort of thin brown
trellis. In many places, damp had entered and discoloured
the paper, making it darker, and frequently leaving patterns and tide marks upon it. In other places, the paper
had peeled away from the wall or had been pulled from it;
in the blank places where it had been, the bricks were revealed to have been whitewashed. The whitewash had
been applied many years ago; it fell from the walls when
they were touched, like pollen from overloaded flowers;

and where it had fallen the bricks were revealed in their original state, except that now they were a faded orange. Their dust lay orange on the floor, and over S's few possessions.

Here and there, S had made his own attempt to decorate the room. In the rear wall, situated only half a metre above the floor, was a square window scarcely bigger than a man's hand; above this window had been pasted a large travel poster printed to advertise a Belgian airline. The name of this airline had been cut from the bottom of the poster, so that the only words remaining on it were Fly To Tahiti. Above these words was a picture of a beach of golden sand, curving unbrokenly into the distance. On the landward side of this beach, tall palms with feathery topknots grew; to seaward, lines of white breakers swept towards the shore; above the beach, a solitary sea bird punctuated an expanse of sky that filled half the area of the poster without revealing a cloud. On the beach, two lovers lay under a bright beach umbrella. The artist's viewpoint was from above (as it might be from a Belgian airliner circling for a landing); the umbrella was tilted back, so that the faces of the lovers could be seen underneath; their faces were two ovals of brown, featureless when examined closely except for small white chips to represent smiling mouths. The picture was dimmed by a covering of dust; some of the dust was a fine orange powder.

To the cross-beam just above S's head as he sat on the log was nailed another invented scene, executed in an artist mode differing greatly from that of the travel poster. This picture was framed in a simple wooden frame to the back of which a metal device was affixed; this device raised a loop of metal above the back of the frame, and it was through the loop that the picture had been nailed so that it hung against the cross-beam.

Reproduced in black and white, the picture bore a legend in the white margin below it which read: W. H. HUNT; The Hireling Shepherd (Oil, 1851). Two figures were depicted in a sunlit rural scene. The left-hand figure was the hireling shepherd whose flock of sheep waited in the background. The hireling shepherd had caught a death's head moth and appeared to be displaying this insect to the second figure, a girl who sat with a lamb upon her lap. The hireling shepherd leant close against her to demonstrate his capture; since the girl with the lamb on her lap appeared to have removed one of her outer garments, the nature of their past, present, and future relationships was ambiguous. The girl looked over her right shoulder with an expression that also was ambiguous. Her mouth appeared pale, with an ample lower lip that perhaps pouted slightly; her eyelids drooped as she looked askance at the man. On some occasions it seemed to S that she regarded the hireling shepherd with a sort of indolent contempt, on other occasions that her expression was one of lazy complaisance.

When S had looked at this for some while, he turned to the round window, knelt, and peered out of it. Pale sunshine lay over the garden now. He looked across the asparagus beds at the house. On the step below the back door was a small white object.

To the right of the round window, a vertical line of bricks had been omitted when the old brick building was built, forming a small niche. Without removing his gaze from the house, S stretched out his right hand and thrust it into the niche. His outstretched fingers met only the brickwork at the back of the niche.

'Where the. . . .'

Removing his gaze from the house, S turned to look in the niche; as he did so, he caught sight of the telescope lying extended under the round window. He picked it up and applied the eyepiece to his right eye, steadying the instrument with both hands as he directed it towards the house.

Into the circle of vision moved the end of the asbestos and concrete garage; it slipped away to the right; a shrub entered the circle briefly, and then a coal bunker, attached to the south corner of the house, and then the long windows of the dining-room, and then the green back door. The circle of vision sank and stopped. In its centre there now rested a full milk bottle, topped by a silver foil cap and standing on the left of the step below the back door.

The circle of vision remained still. In its centre rested the milk bottle; also visible was a part of the step, greyey white, a portion of the brickwork of the house, with its texture of bricks broken by the lines of cement between. In the upper right quarter of the circle was the bottom left corner of the back door, green, closed. Through the four lenses of the telescope, the colours were dull and distorted. On the step, on the extreme limit of vision to the right, lay a dead leaf; through the telescope it appeared black. Apart from these objects, everything else was swallowed in the blackness that lay beyond the circle of vision.

The milk bottle had sloping shoulders. It appeared to have been filled with milk to within about two centimetres of the silver foil cap. It stood on the step. The step was a greyish white, distance rendering it textureless. Where it faded into the blackness, a sort of chromatic effect appeared, a rim of several bright colours dividing the circle of vision from the blackness. The step was not entirely level. Because the milk bottle stood on an uneven step, it was perhaps not standing absolutely straight. The silver foil cap seemed to come to within about ten centimetres of the extreme bottom left tip of the closed door. The door was still closed.

After some while, the dead leaf moved slightly along the step towards the milk bottle. Possibly it was not so much black as a dark brown. It looked shapeless. It lay directly below the corner of the door, on a line with the vertical crack between the door and the jamb. The circle of vision moved slightly, so that this vertical crack lay at its centre. The milk bottle now stood on the left of the circle, near the darkness.

The circle began to tremble. S put down the telescope, resting it still extended on the floor under the round window. He rubbed his eyes with both hands. He stretched his arms above his head. His mouth opened, his head lolled backward, as he yawned. He bent forward, picked up the telescope again, and applied it to his eye.

Bare asparagus beds, a strip of lawn, fled past. A white bottle appeared and the view steadied. The bottle slipped to the left of the circle of vision, so that into the centre of the circle came the vertical crack between door and door jamb. Below it lay a dark dead leaf, shapeless on a grey step. After some while the leaf slid along the step and vanished into the darkness.

After a further while, the vertical crack between door and door jamb widened. The circle of vision became active, moving over a small radius to take in a human foot that protruded from the now opening door. The foot landed on the step, shod in a shoe of a brown material and finished with a high and tapering heel. From the foot rose a slender leg, soon concealed beneath a light blue skirt; an angle further up the skirt revealed where a knee was positioned beneath it. This smoothly curving angle became more noticeable as a hand came into view some distance from it. This hand was a left one, sporting on its fourth finger two rings which gleamed as the hand moved below the level of the knee, down, and curled round the neck of the milk bottle just above the sloping shoulders. The hand tightened its grip, lifted the bottle, raised it beyond the level of the bended knee, which unbent as the bottle was withdrawn from sight of the watcher. The delicately shod foot was withdrawn from the step. It disappeared behind the door. The door closed. A vertical line remained between door and door jamb, pointing down to an empty greyish white step.

2

The right hand with its five soiled nails came up and pinched S's nose at the bridge between his eyes. He screwed up his face and blinked.

He sat down on the planking of the floor of the old brick building with his legs partly under him, resting his right shoulder against the part of the wall adjacent to the round window. Gradually, his head sank back until it also rested against the brickwork. The brickwork here was whitewashed; some grains of the whitewash came down and spread in a fine powder over the hair. The right hand remained over the face, now resting over the eyes and the eyebrows.

After a lapse of time, the legs moved, taking up a fresh pattern on the floor. The right hand remained over the eyes and eyebrows and partially covered the nose. The left hand pressed against the rough wood of the floor, its arm supporting some of the weight of the torso. Gradually the torso leaned further over this left hand, until its position had to be changed, whereupon the left arm bent, moving upwards until the lower section of it slipped up onto the ledge under the round window. The elbow now touched the wood of the window casement, while the hand dangled in air. The right hand remained covering the eyes.

When a measure of time had gone by, this right hand came down from its sheltering gesture on the face to rest lightly on the right thigh.

S now opened his eyes and stared ahead.

Outside the old brick building, a fluttering and scraping noise could be heard. This noise communicated itself to the small section of planking directly over S's head, turning into a more persistent scratching sound as a pigeon entered the small loft provided behind the pigeon holes in the brickwork. S remained staring ahead, giving no sign that he heard these noises. Once he raised his right hand to rub his cheek with his palm.

Slowly his gaze began to move over the room. It fastened on a picture framed and hung on the cross-beam nearest to him.

'Oh Jeanette. . . . If only I could make you understand. . . .'

The picture was a representation in black and white of a man and woman in a rural setting. In the background might be seen a flock of sheep and a cornfield bathed in sun, the two divided by a grassy lane shaded by willows growing on either side of it. In the foreground, on a bank covered with flowers, were two people, depicted at a moment which left their motives for ever in some ambiguity. One of these figures was a country girl. On her knee rested a lamb and two apples; two more apples lay beside her. It could be presumed that the girl was feeding or attempting to feed the lamb with the apples.

The girl had been interrupted in her task by the second figure, a young shepherd dressed in the fustian of a bygone age. He leant confidentially over the girl's shoulder after having scrambled up the bank; his left cheek appeared to rest against the girl's hair which, being long and unconfined, lay over each shoulder.

After regarding these two representations of people for some while, S rose to his feet and moved closer to the picture; he began to examine it at eye level. He breathed on the glass so that the two representations were obscured, lifted his left arm, and rubbed the glass with the cuff of the left sleeve of his shirt.

The picture was now clearly visible through the glass. In the foreground, the two persons sprawled on a flower-covered bank, their bodies forming a sort of inverted V, with their heads together at the top of the V, for while the shepherd was on the left of the central axis of the picture, kneeling and leaning forward, the girl with the lamb on her lap was sitting on the right of the central axis of the picture and leaning backwards; the girl was supporting the weight of her torso by a right arm thrust backwards until the hand had come to rest at a point further to the left than an imaginary straight line dropped from her shoulder, with the result that this arm took up a diagonal that nearly matched the diagonal of the shepherd's body, against which it seemed lightly to rest.

If there was anything behind this phenomenon, if it was not its own lesson, then it could be interpreted to mean that although the girl in part leant away from, or was averse to, the advances of the shepherd, there was nevertheless a part of her that inclined towards him, or was predisposed to accept his advances.

'I wonder if she ever let him . . . or is going to let him . . . if she. . . .'

This ambiguity could hardly be resolved by a scrupulous examiner, since the rest of the picture seemed to echo rather than resolve the ambiguity. (In the same way, the scrupulous examiner was unable to decide permanently whether the creator of the picture had marshalled his objects with a deliberate attempt at a discomforting ambiguity or obliquity of statement, or whether he had aimed at making some form of statement incapable of paraphrase and perhaps not previously attempted, and in so aiming had not entirely succeeded, lapsing instead into an ambiguity that was unwished for.)

It was open to interpretation whether the shepherd was intent upon becoming more intimate with the girl, or whether his absorption was in the collection of lepidoptera: for he leant forward clutching gently in his left hand a large death's head moth which he thrust forward over the girl's left shoulder for her to inspect. Either he had brought this creature as a pretty thing that might serve as a pretext for becoming more intimate with her (and the possessiveness of his pose suggested this alternative) or else he was more concerned with the fine specimen that he had managed, surely with some skill, to capture intact (and the solemnity of his gaze at the moth favoured this alternative). This latter interpretation seemed the less likely, since shepherds, whose associations with nature render them unsurprised by its manifestations, rarely become lepidopterists. On the other hand, this particular moth, fine specimen though it was, represented an unfortunate choice of a bauble with which to lull the girl's apprehensions, since superstitions attaching to the death's head moth would make it an object of unease to such a simple country person as the girl depicted.

In any event, the girl was not regarding the moth. She had turned her head away from it, though whether this was from a revulsion for the moth or because in so doing she could have a close look at the face of the shepherd, virtually resting on her left shoulder, remained in doubt.

'Really,' said Domoladossa, *'this is too bad! Here is this long and increasingly pedantic description of a mediocre painting hanging in the coach house. What's more, it has already been described once, and that was quite enough. Such an item must be quite irrelevant to our main interest.'*

'Do you think so?' Midlakemela said neutrally.

'I do think so! Don't you?'

Midlakemela shrugged and inclined his head. In a moment, he excused himself and went over to the Governor's office.

'Any news?'

'Not really, sir. But there is one curious item which has just come up. Domoladossa doesn't think it important, but I believe it ought to be mentioned to you, sir.'

'Well?'

'It's a picture, sir, hanging in the loft above the coach

house where S is hiding. From its description, it might well be the same picture that G has hanging in his wooden bungalow, which the report describes only briefly and in general terms. We're getting a much more ample report of it now. It seems to me a bit fishy that the same picture should hang in both places.'

'I don't see why, Midlakemela. What is this picture?'

'It's a shepherd and his girl friend, sir. Evidently in a rather promiscuous situation. Could we check on it? It appears it was painted by a W. H. Hunt, and is called The Hireling Shepherd.'

The Governor rubbed his nose. 'Never heard of him.'

He called a subordinate and despatched him scurrying for an encyclopaedia. The subordinate returned, leafing through a fat volume, finally to read aloud with an air of triumph:

'"Winkel Henri Hunt (1822–1887). Russian-born German of British extraction, b. at St Petersburg. Displayed from childhood equal liking for art and science. Professional career that of expert chemist, all spare time devoted to painting and bear-shooting. First canvases show influence of Fuseli. . . . Well known portraits of such musicians as Gazakirski and Borodin, with whom v. friendly. Discovered hunterine oxide (1850); best-known paintings include On the Steps of the Winter Palace (1846), Death of Attila (1849) and The Hireling Shepherd (1851). Married in 1859, Countess—".

'Enough!' said the Governor. 'Well, Midlakemela, the painter exists in our probability-world, just as in Probability A. It is something to go on, I suppose. But as to why both G and S should have copies of one of his pictures. . . .'

The girl's face was oval. It did not appear particularly intelligent, nor particularly pretty; yet it was not unattractive. The two eyes were large and set widely apart; they lay under heavy, even puffy, lids, while the lower lids were also noticeable. Above these lids were broad soft eyebrows, untouched by art. The nose seemed not too long and rather soft, and on the whole attractive nose, ending in a little soft bulb of flesh. The mouth too looked attractive in texture, though the broad lower lip gave it something of a pout; if it was pouting, there was no reason within the context of the picture not to suppose that the girl was pouting because she mistrusted the advances of the young shepherd. The look in her eyes could be read as reinforcing this impression, for they glanced sideways at him with an expression which might have been lazy contempt; on the other hand it might easily have been one of indolent complaisance.

It was tantalizing to imagine that the painter could have created a second representation of this same imaginary scene, setting it say fifteen minutes (they would have to be imaginary minutes on an imaginary time scale, since art has little relation to the ordinary clock) ahead of the existing representation. Many doubts could then have been resolved, for one paradox of the existing picture was that its ambiguities were engendered by the fact that it showed only one moment on its time scale. Suppose that the second representation, depicting the same scene some fifteen minutes later, could be produced. It too would only show one moment on its time scale; but by comparison with the earlier moment in the first and existing picture, it would make much clear. For instance, it might show the shepherd some distance away in the middle distance, back tending his sheep; in which case it would be clearer that in the first and existing picture the shepherd's interest lay at least as much in the moth as in possession of the girl, and that the girl's expression contained more lazy contempt than complaisance or concupiscence under the heavy summer lids of her eyes. Or the second picture might show that the warmth of the summer day had worked in these young bodies, and that the more instinctive side of human nature had had its way, that the girl's expression in the first and existing picture might indeed have been sly, but was also full of complicity; for this second picture might depict the sheep untended breaking down the corn, and the flowers of the bank crushed, as the shepherd and the girl became lovers, their bodies lying parallel and together, with that pale, soft, pouting lower lip pressed beneath the man's heavy kisses.

But the imaginary picture remained imaginary, and the existing picture remained open to torturing interpretation.

S turned away, opening his mouth to sigh as he jerked his head to one side. He began to walk up and down the room, avoiding the three cross-beams, going to the far end until his chin was level with a solitary seabird punctuating an expanse of printed blue sky, coming back to the front of the room until his chin was level with a large bunch of flowers separated from other such bunches by a diamond of trellis.

When he had finished his pacing, he took up a sitting posture on a log on the floor from which he could gaze through a round window divided into nine panes of glass, the centre pane of which formed a small square, and commenced to survey the rear of the house that stood on a slight eminence some thirty-five metres away, beyond the bare asparagus beds.

Domoladossa was interrupted in his reading of the report from Probability A by the return of Midlakemela. Accompanying Midlakemela was the Governor, who nodded cordially as Domoladossa rose.

'Don't disturb yourself. I just wanted to hear what your first impressions were.'

Through the photograph of Domoladossa's wife on his desk, the four Distinguishers watching the scene became more alert. The eldest, whose name was Charlock, said, 'Ah, now this man who has just entered bears a strong resemblance to the first man in this dimension we ever observed, when our congruence with it was first discovered. They are entirely unaware of us.'

The youngest present, Corless, said impatiently, 'Well, we can do nothing about it until our Cogitators invent a way of signalling between our dimension and theirs. I still hold to the theory that this . . . manifestation rests on a question of size. We are looking into a sub-atomic world, probably through a temporary distortion in the space-time-infrastructure.'

Charlock began strolling down the hillside and Corless went with him. They were both intellectually fascinated by the phenomenon on the hill, but not emotionally involved; perhaps that might change when they had instruments with which to communicate with the inhabitants of the freak world.

As they walked down the hill, a small robot fly followed

93

them. As vision was transmitted to a vast receiving set in a second-storey hall in New York, a group of men, several of them in uniform, stood or sat watching the transmission.

At a raised dais, a technician under orders from the statesmen present was controlling the flight of the robot fly.

Congressman Sadlier turned to his companion.

'You see, Joe, that's the way it is. We've broken through at last—though what or where we've broken through to remains to be seen.'

'A plurality of worlds . . .', Joe muttered. As a radio communications engineer, he felt he should come up with some bright suggestions; but at the moment only vague poetic associations filtered through his head.

Unaware of his multiple watchers, Domoladossa was showing the Governor the next part of the report.

3

Some while later, a movement distracted S's gaze from the house, causing it to flick over to the left. There, only slightly obscured by the outermost twigs of an apple tree that blossomed late, and the branches of a sumac tree, a wooden bungalow attracted his attention; from the door of the wooden bungalow, a figure was emerging. The figure bore a mat that appeared to have dull-coloured stripes on it. The figure began to shake the mat.

Even from this distance, it could be seen that the head of this figure was turned to look over its left shoulder as if regarding a brown side gate that would be visible to its view while remaining concealed from the watcher behind the west corner of the house. A plump figure appeared from this direction and stopped a couple of metres away from the figure holding the mat. Round the body of the plump figure was wrapped a large coat of a liver colour; the person thus enveloped carried an umbrella, while stockinged legs appeared below the coat to disappear into ankle boots. From this distance it could be discerned that the person had a large head, the hair of which was grey and swept back into a bun behind the head, while on the crown of the head rested a small hat that carried some sort of coloured ornament.

When the two figures had stood within easy talking distance of each other for some while, the figure bearing the mat turned and walked off, heading for the wooden bungalow, which he entered, closing the door behind him. This event set the plump person into motion again. She made for the west corner of the house, gained the concrete path there, and continued on without pausing in her progress until she reached the back door; there she paused only long enough to knock on one of the long green panels before she pulled the door open and entered it, afterwards closing it behind her.

S remained where he was, waiting and watching. His gaze moved from the closed back door to the open kitchen window. The plump person became visible at this opening. She engaged in a complicated manœuvre or series of gestures which removed the liver-coloured coat from her body. Even from a distance, it could be seen that she wore some sort of a white apron below the coat.

She was now periodically visible about the kitchen. Twice she came out of the back door. On the first occasion, she carried a coal scuttle which she took to the bunker on the right of the long windows of the dining-room; setting the scuttle on the ground, she took a shovel from it and with this shovel scooped coal from the bottom of the bunker, throwing it into the scuttle until the scuttle was filled with coal. The sound of this operation could be heard inside the old brick building that was separated from the house by asparagus beds. On the second occasion, the plump figure emerged with a metal can that she carried by a handle on its side. With this article she passed along the back of the house and beyond the coal bunker, altered direction until she walked in a north-easterly direction, so that a pattern of four white ribbons meeting in the middle of her back could be certainly discerned, crossed a stretch of lawn, and reached a door set in the back wall of a garage constructed mainly of asbestos, reinforced by pillars of concrete. The plump person entered this door, closing it behind her when she was inside the garage, and remaining there for some while before re-emerging with her can. By comparing the way she walked back over the grass, past the coal bunker, and back to the back door, with her left arm stretching down towards the can it carried and her right arm stiff and extended at an angle of about thirty degrees from her body, it could be deduced that she had transported the can empty to the garage, had filled it inside the garage, and now bore it back full into the house.

S turned his head away from the window. By his feet lay a copy of a boys' magazine printed some years ago when S himself had been a boy. The pages were yellow with age. They lay open at a picture of a big bearded man with glaring eyeballs wielding an oar above his head; he stood in the threshold of a doorway beyond which, lying in a corner of a bare room, was a schoolboy

97

with his hands and feet tied together with rope. The boy still wore his school cap. Above this picture were the words The Secret of the Grey Mill.

Picking the magazine up, S started to read the story. When he had read several sentences, his eye wandered across the page to the next page. Finally it alighted upon a sentence which said, Thirsty though he was, he watched the brackish water drain away without regret. Continuing to read from there, S turned the page. He read to the bottom of the page. There, a passage in black type said, Who is trapped down the old well? Do not miss next week's gripping episode. S closed the magazine and placed it on the log that lay near at hand. He looked out of the round window, saw no movement in the garden or through the windows of the house, and so brought his gaze back inside the old brick building, letting it rest on the floor.

The planks were uneven and tawny in colour. The raised parts of the planks, particularly where a knot lay exposed in the wood, were a lighter colour than the rest. In the bottom of the small indentations in the planks, the wood was often darkened by a collection of dirt.

S glanced up occasionally from the floor to look out of the window. If nothing attracted his attention, he looked down at the floor again. Sometimes he traced an imaginary pattern among the knots and grooves.

He glanced out of the round window and saw that someone was coming towards the old brick building in which he sat.

Rising to his knees, S concealed his body behind the brickwork before allowing his head to move forward so that he could again look through the round window that was divided into nine sections. The plump person in the white apron was carrying a bucket in which some sort of green substance could be glimpsed. She had crossed over the stretch of lawn before the back door, and was progressing down a narrow dirt path that ran parallel with the asparagus bed, fringing the bed to its south-east side just as the gravel walk did on its north-west side. This path led under screening fruit trees adjacent to the south-east wall of the old brick building before terminating at a rubbish tip lying almost against a privet hedge that bounded Mr. Mary's property on the south-west side. To get to this rubbish tip, it was necessary for anyone walking along the dirt path to come near to the front of the old brick building, and to pass in fact within touching distance of its east corner.

When the plump person got to within three metres of this corner, she stopped and looked up at the round window set in the upper part of the front of the old coach house, above the two doors with their worn grey timber.

'Are you up there? Hoy, wake up, it's only me. Are you up there?'

'Where is he?'

'Oh, there you are! Why don't you come down? I bet you were asleep.'

'Is he in?'

'He's in his study with the door shut and a pen in his hand and Lord knows what mighty thoughts in his head.'

'I wasn't asleep, Vi. Are you sure?'

'You know as well as I do. . . . Why don't you come down? I bet you were asleep.'

'She?'

'I've got work to do. She's gone out shopping with her basket and umbrella and new coat.'

'Smart, eh?'

'Very smart this morning, we are. All dolled up this morning. Are you coming down or aren't you?'

'I'm just coming.'

Going to the other end of the room, S bent down and lifted up a trapdoor that he rested back against the rear wall of the building in which was a small window set close to the floor. A solid wooden structure of steps was revealed. S went down them, turning the corner and descending over a further seven treads until his feet touched the cobbles that formed the floor of the old coach house. Here the light was dim; gleams of light filtered through vertical and horizontal cracks in the two timber doors at the front of the building, and through the windows set in the timber doors.

In one of these two doors, the left one as S faced them, a small door no higher than one and a half metres had been fitted. Cracks of light appeared round it also.

'Come on, then, let's be having you. I haven't got all day.'

'You'll work yourself into an early grave.'

Into the ancient timbers of the left-hand door, a nail had been knocked close to the small inserted door. A loop of cord hung round this nail; the other end of this cord was tied round the end of a nut securing the handle of the little door, which was on the outside of the little door. S took the loop off the nail and pushed the door open.

He blinked and stuck his head out. He looked up at the house, and then at the plump woman.

'Are you coming then? I haven't got all day. I wouldn't mind betting you were asleep.'

S emerged from the small door, straightened, and took a pace nearer to the plump woman.

Her large figure consisted of a series of interdependent curves. S's figure was composed mainly of straight lines. An uninformed viewer seeing these two figures would have been surprised to learn that both figures were supported internally by two skeletons not at all unlike.

The plump woman was dressed in a grey dress; over it was a large white apron that had two ribbons to secure it round the waist and two more ribbons that sprouted from the top of the apron, above the swell of the breast, to secure it over the shoulders. The plump woman's hair was also secured by a piece of velvet ribbon. The hair was a yellowy grey, drawn back to the back of the head, where it was dressed into a bun. The woman's face was pale, with only an irregular patch of colour in either cheek. Her eyes, of a washed blue, were bolstered on noticeably large underlids that swelled into folds of flesh with pasty shadows beneath them.

'Are you sure he's working?'

'At this time of morning? It's write, write, write, even when you take his coffee in.'

'Is he advertising for a new secretary?'

'What, after you? How are you? You don't look too good. You're a fool, you are, really, nice young chap like you. You're wasting your time.'

'Don't get on at me, Vi.'

'I'm not getting on at you, but really—I mean, suppose everyone in the world went round getting funny ideas, I mean, where'd we all be, eh?'

'They say there's been a strike at the fish factory.'

'Do they, now? And who told you that? You really don't look too good, you know. Look at your eyes!'

'Watt told me.'

'Which fish factory was this?'

'You'd better ask him. He told me.'

'You don't want to trust all Watt tells you. He can't tell you the time correctly.'

'The place where they can the fish, I suppose.'

'Don't be so daft. There's no such place. Not round here, anyway.'

S looked down at his shoes; they were covered with grey dust. Gravel was trodden into dark brown earth, lying under his shoes.

'Did you bring me anything?'

'I shouldn't do it. Really I shouldn't. I'm daft to do it.'

From the top of the pail she carried, the plump woman brushed aside some outer leaves of cabbage and produced a bundle of newspaper. She held it out to S. He stepped forward and took it, remaining there awkwardly looking at her.

'It's half a pork pie. I shouldn't do it, Lord knows, but they'll never miss it.'

'You're terribly kind.'

'Let's not go into all that again. You know me by now. What I do I do. Why don't you come in and have a bath?'

'What, in the house? With him just in his study? He'd shoot me.'

'Don't talk so bloody daft. He won't stir till lunch time. You need a bath. You know you need a bath.'

'I don't need a bath. Imagine me creeping into that

house! Besides, suppose she came back and caught me in the bath!'

The plump woman laughed.

'Go on with you, you men are all the same, you know you'd love it.'

'He'd shoot me if he saw me!'

'Well, I can't stay here all day. Some of us have got work to do if others haven't.'

'Could you bring me a drop of paraffin for my lamp, please, Vi?'

'I tell you, you men are all the same, nothing but a nuisance. Fetch us your lamp, then. Why you can't go and fill it yourself. . . .'

'You know why.'

The plump woman stood where she was until S disappeared through the small door set in the large doors of the old brick building. Then she moved forward again along the dirt path, ducked her head as she went under the bare bough of an apple tree, and shot the contents of her white enamelled bucket out onto the top of the rubbish tip. When she returned to the spot where she had been standing before, she waited there until S returned to her. In his hand he carried a rusty storm lantern; he raised it and gave it to her.

'I'll bring it back when I can. I've got a lot to do this morning. She wants me to do them scallops of veal for lunch. She's gone out to get some anchovy now.'

'Goodbye. Thank you for the pork pie.'

'I'm a fool, that's what I am.'

S stood and watched the four ribbons involved in a bow where they met in the centre of the back. The white pail, now empty, which the plump woman carried in her right hand, was brighter than the colour of the apron; the ends of the ribbons were creased, and somewhat yellowed. In a brief while, the woman reached the back door, which she had left ajar; she climbed the step and went through the door; as it closed behind her, S turned and climbed back through the small door into the old brick building.

4

When S regained the room above the coach house, he let down the trapdoor and advanced into the middle of the room. The newspaper parcel which he had been clutching he placed on one of the shelves that ran along the south-east side of the room, next to a small brass crocodile.

Hanging on a level with his chest was a hammock made of canvas, its two ends threaded with ropes that ran out to two of the low cross-beams, looping through two thick metal rings that hung over two nails knocked into the first and second of the three cross-beams. Drooping over the two sides of this hammock were the corners of two grey blankets, their edges bound up with red wool, and an arrangement of sacks strung or stitched together with garden twine. Placing his two arms inside the hammock, S bent his knees and sprang upwards, hauling himself into the hammock.

When he was in the hammock, and it had ceased to swing, he sat up and untied the laces of his shoes. Removing first the left shoe and then the right, he dropped them down onto the floor, where the indentations on the planking formed an arrangement of shades, some almost straw-coloured, some more of a dark sienna shade where dirt had rubbed into the wood; the effect to an unfocused eye was reminiscent of a woman's hair. The two shoes rolled and lay together, their toecaps touching, at an angle of ninety degrees; the left shoe lay with its sole exposed. The sole was worn in the middle and frayed round the sides. The toecap of the right shoe was battered. The two shoes lay together. They formed a chance arrangement on the floor. Underneath them ran the tawny planks of the floor. They touched the floor at a number of points; they touched each other at the toes. The shoes lay directly below the downward-directed eye of the man, until he turned away and lay down.

Beneath his head, S arranged more comfortably a small body that served him as pillow. This body, which was beige in colour, had attached to it a head made to represent a species of bear. The representation was less exact than it had been when the animal was newly fashioned, since it lacked both ears and an eye. The body also had undergone a change with age; not only had its contours been flattened and softened; its arms and legs were lost, their former positions being indicated by four holes in the beige material through which woody and fibrous stuffing protruded. The man arranged this object to serve as a pillow, pressing his head back against the flaccid stomach of the bear, so that its head nodded above his own, and appeared to stare into the room with its one remaining brown glass eye.

The man's gaze rested upon the roofing above him, where many parallel rough hewn beams ran down from the thick centre beam to the side walls, supporting curling orange tiles. Some of the tiles were chipped; some had slipped from their original position. Light spread between the tiles, coming in the cracks and widening into bands of bright whiteness that tended to obscure the tiles.

The man's gaze became more diffused. His eyelids descended over his eyes and he slept.

Once he moved in his sleep, turning his head towards his right shoulder. The movement caused the bear to move its head slightly too. His breathing became slower and more grating as it passed over his dry palate; its susurration was audible in the silent room.

When he woke, his gaze took in a stove that stood near the central cross-beam. It was black, although on its grills, vents, slides, spinwheels, patent pokers, and other protrusions rested a thin film of dust that was light grey in colour.

S swung two stockinged feet over the side of the hammock and slid to the floor, planting his feet on the planking a few centimetres from his shoes. He sat on the floor and put the shoes onto his feet. He laced the shoes. He stood up and went to the front of the room, where a round window, intersected by four strips of wood placed two one way and two another dividing the circle into nine segments, the middle one square, was let into the brickwork of the wall. Stooping, he peered out of this window.

Below and in front of this window was an asparagus bed, made up into three long mounds which were bare now except for a number of weeds growing on them, fringed on one side by a gravel walk and on the other by a dirt path. The gravel walk was fringed on its other side by a low privet hedge. Along the gravel walk was strutting a pigeon known as X which thrust its neck and head forward with each step it took. Beyond the asparagus bed lay a strip of lawn that led, in its north-westerly continuation, towards the vegetable and fruit garden and, in its south-easterly direction, towards the flower garden. Beyond this strip of lawn, built on ground slightly higher than the ground on which stood the old brick building that had once been called a coach house by property holders of an earlier epoch, was the plain square house with some of the panes of glass in its windows gleaming in the sunshine. On the first floor, the window on the right belonged to the bathroom. Through this window only a blankness could be seen; it was a light blankness since the bathroom had two windows, the one unseen being round the corner of the south-east side of the house. To the left of the bathroom window were two windows belonging to two spare rooms. There was no movement in them. S blinked his eyes, yawned, and surveyed the windows on the ground floor. Below the left of the two spare room windows was the kitchen window. Resting on the sill inside the middle portion of this window was a can that threw off a gleam in the sunshine; the two side portions of the window were open. No movement could be detected in the kitchen. The back door stood next to the kitchen window. A cat covered with black and white fur lay sunning itself on the step beneath the door; the door was closed. To the right of the back door was the dining-room window, a long window reaching to the ground which could be opened to admit people to the garden. Like the bathroom above it, this room also possessed a second window, concealed from view round the corner on the south-east wall of the house. In the light received through these two windows, it was possible to make out a figure garbed at least partially in white moving round a table only partly in view and doing something with or to the table.

Turning away from the round window, S walked to the other end of the room, avoiding the three low crossbeams and moving between the black iron stove and the hammock. Set in the floor at the other end of the room was a trapdoor made of the same sort of wood as the floor, though less worn than the floor. S lifted this trapdoor and climbed down the steps that were revealed beneath it. He emerged into a dim and dusty room, the cobbled floor of which was encumbered by a variety of objects. As S passed a work bench on his left, he passed on his right a stack of old timber, a lawn mower, a number of boxes of varying shapes and sizes, some broken pieces of furniture, including an old wash-hand stand with a cracked marble top, a tin trunk with a domed lid on which had been painted the initials H.S.M., a garden roller, a large kitchen mangle of an obsolete variety, a rusty bird cage, and various other objects, including a row of garden tools standing or leaning against the wall. S advanced to two old timber doors that formed the north-east side of the old building; they had slumped on their hinges, so that their lower edges touched the ground; some of their panels had shrunk, so that chinks of light could filter through horizontal and vertical cracks.

In the left hand of these two doors was set a smaller door, which S now opened slightly. Thrusting his head forward, he peered out towards the south-east corner of the building, close to which ran the course of a dirt path leading from further up the garden to a rubbish tip set behind trees. At that point grew a thin and gnarled trunk, rising from the ground to branch out higher up into a voluminous ivy partly covering that side of the old building. Close to the gnarled trunk stood a rusty storm lantern.

Opening the small door further, S stepped through it, putting his feet on the ground and moving towards the storm lantern; as he went, he looked across his left shoulder up at the house. In the dining-room window, he saw a movement. Someone was watching him from behind the dining-room curtains.

Without reaching the lantern, S turned round and moved back to the small door; he climbed through it without hesitation and moved back through the dismal coach house with its forsaken objects grouped mainly on his left hand. Against the rear wall, a sturdy wooden staircase led to the room above. S ran up the stairs, climbed into the room, and let down a trapdoor over the stair well. Ducking his head, he moved forward again, avoiding three low beams that ran across the space from wall to wall, passing on his left an old stove bearing on its lid an inscription wrought from the iron that read Stentorian 1888 (these words almost encircled the lid) and on his right a hammock secured from two of the low beams.

A round window, crossed by two horizontal and two vertical bars so as to divide it into nine panes, the centre pane of which was square, was set in the front wall of the building. Dropping down onto his knees, S pressed against the brickwork to the right of the round window. At that point, a recess gave into the wall; plunging his hand into the recess, S drew from it a folded telescope some fifteen centimetres long and bound in leather. The leather was worn and soft. Pulling at this telescope with both hands, S extended it until three brass sections appeared. In the smallest section was an eyepiece. Placing the telescope so that it pointed unobtrusively out of one of the small side panes of glass, S applied his right eye to the eyepiece.

Moving his left hand, which held the telescope by the leather binding, S trained the telescope's circle of vision onto the house. Its brickwork appeared, red and fuzzy. After a slight pressure on the end of the instrument, the fuzziness dissolved into a pattern of oblong bricks surrounded by broken vertical and continuous horizontal lines of concrete. The circle of vision moved across the pattern until from the darkness outside it emerged the long windows of the dining-room.

Inside the dining-room could be seen the corner of a table spread with a white cloth; objects could be distinguished lying on the cloth. A good deal of light filled the dining-room, flowing into it not only from this window but from a second window round the corner on the south-east side of the house. By this light it was possible to distinguish that the long drapes hanging on either side

of the two windows which could be opened onto the
garden were of a green colour. It could also be distinguished that from behind the left of the two drapes protruded, at the lower part, a shoe and a section of leg
clad in some dark suiting, and, at the middle part, a
shoulder, clothed in the same dark suiting, and, possibly,
murkily, just above the shoulder, the left side of a face.
The circle of vision became unsteady. In consequence,
definition of detail became more difficult, but it seemed
as if fingers—something of the lightness of flesh—clutched
at the drape on a level with the protruding shoulder.

The circle of vision took on a flutter, so that as it
travelled involuntarily in a small arc it also encompassed
brief glimpses of the bathroom window above, and of
the grass below the long dining-room window. The left-
hand drape inside the window did not move.

Removing the telescope from his eye, S steadied his
left arm by resting the elbow on the brick ledge beneath
the round window and by pressing the wrist against the
brick at the side of the window. He applied his eye once
more to the eyepiece of the optical instrument, in time
to catch a movement in the dining-room window. The
left-hand drape had been released. It settled back into
position. No other movement could be seen in the room.

S removed the telescope from his right eye and placed
it on the flooring directly under the round window, almost touching the wall.

'Oh, Vi, if you've been telling him. . . .'

S rose to his feet. He patted his knees, then sank until
he was on them. Ensuring that his body was not exposed
to the window, he looked out of one of the side panes
towards the house.

'I don't know what I'd do. . . .'

Blue sky interspersed with cloud was behind the house. The roof of the house was covered with grey-blue slates, while the angles of the roof were capped by lines of stone. The roof tree was capped by a similar line of stone and was terminated at each end by an ornamental stone urn that stood out against the sky. A wide chimney stack containing six tubby pottery chimneys rose from this side of the roof. Below the line of the roof ran a rain gutter. At the two visible corners of the house, drainpipes met this guttering and ran down straight to the ground. The brickwork of the rear of the house was interspersed by five windows and a door. Three of these windows were on the first floor, the right-hand window belonging to a bathroom that possessed a second window round the corner on the south-east wall of the house. Beneath the visible bathroom window was a window comprising two long doors which could be opened by anyone inside the room, to give them access to the garden. On either side of this long window hung long curtains; the curtains did not move. Neither the curtain on the left nor the curtain on the right of the long window stirred, nor could any movement, nor any figure or part of a figure be discerned in the room. The room was a dining-room; the part of it visible to the watcher seemed to be empty. Nothing animate appeared in it. The two long glass doors were divided in all into sixteen panes; through none of the panes could any person or any part of any person be detected.

The other window set in the lower storey of the house belonged to the kitchen. Unlike the other windows, it had a steel frame, divided into three sections. The two outer sections were open. Within the kitchen, a predominantly white figure could be seen moving about.

'I don't know what I'd do.'

The white figure was not always visible. Most of the time she was poorly visible at the back of the kitchen, when her presence was more inferred than seen; at other times she moved to a part of the kitchen where she could not be observed at all. Once she bent down so that she could not be seen in a part of the room where she was normally visible.

S blinked his eyes.

His legs were doubled under him, so that he sat on the tawny planking with the following parts of his anatomy touching it: some of his right buttock, the outer side of his right thigh, his right knee, the outer side of his right calf, his right ankle, and his right foot, while his left leg copied the attitude of his right one, overlapping it so that from the knee down it also touched the planking and the tip of the left shoe pressed against the heel of the right shoe. The shoes were dusty. His right shoulder and a part of the right-hand side of his body pressed against the brickwork beside the round window.

He stared into the corner ahead of him, where the sloping beams of the roof met the front wall of the old building. There, on the front wall, was hung some wallpaper with a pattern of bunches of flowers separated from each other by a pattern of trellis. The corner of the paper nearest the beams had peeled away from the wall and hung curling and discoloured over the rest of the paper. A spider worked its way over one of the discoloured bunches of flowers.

Turning his head away, S looked out of the round

114

window. Running from a point somewhere below the window or slightly to its left was a gravel walk which went towards the house; this walk was boarded with a privet hedge. The privet was not uniformly in good condition all the way along the walk; at one place, some metres from the old brick building, the bushes which comprised it became straggling. Behind the straggling part was a cat covered with black and white fur. It crouched with its head low to the ground and its ears back on its head; its rump, which was raised higher than its head, supported a tail which twitched first to the right and then to the left in slow deliberate movements. Its eyes were fixed on a point roughly a metre and a quarter further down the walk, and thus nearer to the old brick building than the cat. At this point was a pigeon, moving with a waddle in erratic circle, pecking at the ground with its beak. Its legs and feet were red; round one of its legs it wore a ring of a metal resembling pewter. Its body was covered with white and grey feathers.

In one of the windows of the house, a movement could be detected. The woman clad mainly in white had left the kitchen. Her form now appeared through the long window of the dining-room. She moved about the table. She then disappeared, but later became visible once more through the left-hand open section of the kitchen window.

It could be seen that a second person was in the kitchen, not moving, and seeming to rest partially against the table in the middle of the room. The upper half only of this person was visible; it was covered in a blue garment that appeared to be a cardigan. The person had hair partly concealing her face as she turned towards the woman clad in white, who was active in one corner of the kitchen. The woman in the blue garment moved to the other side of the table, the side nearer the window, and leant with her back against the sink with her hands behind her back touching one another.

Still directing his gaze through the round window, S leant his body back from the brickwork. His right arm had been covering a niche in the brickwork. He brought up his left hand and felt with it into this niche. When his fingers encountered the brickwork at the back of the niche, he looked away from the window into the niche. The niche was empty. On the floor just below the round window, resting with its four sections extended, was a brass telescope. S picked it up and directed it towards the window. As he did so, he glanced into a part of the garden near at hand and saw that a fat pigeon waddled on the gravel walk, its head and neck thrusting forward with every step it took. Behind it, partly concealed behind a stretch of privet hedge, was a black and white cat, crouching with its skull low on its front paws and its ears flat against its skull.

Placing the eyepiece of the telescope to his eye, S directed it up the garden to survey the kitchen window. Through the middle panel of the window could be seen a woman's head; the woman was looking away from the window into the room. Between her head and the eye of the watcher were interposed the glass of the kitchen window, the glass of the round window in the old brick building that had once housed a gentleman's private coach, and the four lenses of the telescope. Her hair curled upwards from her neck, was combed upwards, and secured low on the back of her head with an ornamental comb. Her right hand had been removed from behind her back; she waved it gently, bent at the elbow, with the fingers pointing upwards and untensed. Beside the table, near to her and visible through the open right-hand side of the window, was a plump woman in a white apron. The plump woman had her hands resting on her hips. It could be seen that occasionally her lips moved.

The two women began to alter their positions. Their movements could be seen in the circle of vision. The woman in a white apron went to the left side of the kitchen and bent down. When she straightened, she was seen to bear a large dish in her two hands. She placed this on the table and then again bent down on the left side of the room. The other woman moved to the table bearing a tray. She put the tray on the table. She picked up the large dish and placed it on the tray. On the large dish, golden brown objects could be seen. The woman with the tawny hair picked up the tray and turned with it, moving until she was hidden by the frame of the window and the brickwork adjoining.

The circle of vision moved to the right, gliding over the brickwork of the house, leaving the kitchen window behind in the darkness beyond the circle. It passed across a door in which gleamed a small square of green glass, across more brickwork, and reached a long window, the sides of which were bordered inside by curtains of a green material; these curtains did not move.

As the circle of vision settled, the woman with tawny hair came into view, bearing before her a plate on a tray. She went to a corner of the room, where her movements were lost, turned, and placed the plate on the table. She moved out of sight. Almost at once, a plump woman came into view bearing a tray; on the tray, dishes could be distinguished. They became lost to view as the plump woman moved to a corner of the room. She turned and distributed the dishes on the table before her. From the edge of the table hung a white cloth. At the end of the table nearest to the window, a chair was placed; its legs curled slightly, as did its back. At the other end of the table, the watcher could just distinguish part of the back of another chair rising above the table top.

When the woman had distributed the dishes, she turned again to the corner of the room at which she had previously busied herself. She took two trays into her hands and left the room.

A man dressed in dark suiting came into view. The woman with the tawny hair swept up into a curve on the back of her head followed him. The man came towards the window. As he did so, he shot a glance out of the window and down the garden. For an appreciable moment of time, he appeared to be looking up the telescope at the eye of the watcher. The circle of vision moved away, swimming over the brickwork and a speeding stretch of garden, and then returning. Six layers of glass were interposed between the watcher in the old building and the man in the dark suiting.

The man in the dark suiting, without pausing at the long window, took hold of the back of the chair near the window, pulled it towards him, and sat down upon it, moving it so that he sat up to the table. The woman followed his example, seating herself at the other end of the table. The table was so placed that the man's head obscured the woman's face. The man had his back to the window. The man had a long dark back. His two hands picked up articles from the table. His elbows began to move.

S put down the telescope without closing it, laying it under the round window on the flooring. He pinched his nose between his eyes, where the bridge was narrowest. He blinked his eyes and looked round the side of the round window, through the glass and up to the house. Through the kitchen window, he could see that the plump woman sat at the table behind the open window. She no longer wore the white apron; as far as could be seen, she wore a grey dress. She leaned over the table. She went through the motions of eating.

'They are eating a meal in the house,' the Governor said.

'Exactly,' Domoladossa said. 'An ordinary meal, an everyday occurrence. Yet who knows if their intestinal flora are as ours? Who can say if the meat they enjoy— veal, isn't it?—would not poison us?'

'There's so much we don't know,' agreed the Governor. 'Meanwhile, all we can do is scrutinize their every movement.'

'If we could get our data more directly,' Midlakemela said. 'If we could only penetrate inside Mr. Mary's house.'

'SHE holds the key to the mystery. I feel it in my bones,' Domoladossa said, reverting to his old hobby horse.

He was being scrutinized by two Distinguishers on a hillside. They, in turn, were being watched by a group of men in a New York building.

Joe Growleth had been working in the room for five hours and was a little weary. Turning to Congressman Sadlier, he said, 'Well, that's how it seems to be. Our robot *fly has materialized into a world where it so happens that the first group of inhabitants we come across is studying another world they have discovered—a world in which the inhabitants they watch are studying a report they have obtained from another world.'*

'I'd say we've run into some kind of mental reflection-distortion effect—hitherto unknown, as they say in the Sunday supplements.'

'Maybe so. Or maybe the key to it all lies in that report. Hey!—Suppose that report comes from the real world! Suppose the guys reading it, and the guys on the hill-side watching them, and us watching THEM, are FALSE worlds, phase echoes. . . . Makes your flesh creep, doesn't it?'

The Congressman said, 'All we are after is facts. We don't have to decide what reality is, thank God!'

Cloud began to thicken over the house. The sun was obscured. Leaves blew across the asparagus bed; some rolled over the tops of the three mounds. To the left of the asparagus bed, a fat pigeon flapped and clattered its wings and rose to perch on a low privet hedge that fringed a gravel walk. Further away from the watcher, a black and white cat rose from behind a stem of privet and stalked away towards the house. Its tail was black, with a white tip at the end of it. The tail was carried high; the white tip twitched gently as the cat walked away. The pigeon rose from the privet hedge to fly awkwardly into an apple tree.

5

The room above the old coach house had for its ceiling an inverted V of dark beams which supported old tiles of a mellow orange. Between the beams were spiders' webs; many of the webs were grey with dust. At the far end of the room was a small square window only a few centimetres above the level of the floor. The room was divided into three by supporting cross-beams of dark wood. The light in the room was dim. Between the two cross-beams nearest to S hung a hammock, made of canvas and suspended by rope. Over the sides of this hammock hung some sacks stitched together with garden twine, the ends of one or more blankets, and part of the face of a toy bear. The bear's nose was indicated with black wool stitched in a square over the beige material

121

of the head. The bear had no mouth. It had one amber eye, which seemed to look down at S.

S rose to his feet and laid the bear so that it did not protrude over the side of the hammock. To do this, he reached over the first of the low cross-beams from which the hammock was suspended. A picture hung on S's side of the beam. His shirt caught the corner of the picture frame, setting it swinging. S stepped back and steadied it.

The picture was in black and white, though behind the glass both the black of the print and the white of the paper were faded. The picture showed a man and a woman touching each other, the man dressed in the garb of a shepherd, the woman in some sort of smock, worn over a skirt; it was not certain that she was not partially undressed. The shepherd was clearly neglecting his sheep, which had begun to stray into a field of corn, to secure the attention of the girl. It was difficult to understand from the picture whether his efforts to interest her were meeting with success, for her look could be read either as scornful or as one of sly desire.

The shepherd was holding out for her inspection a moth of a certain species which he had caught. The girl was looking away from this moth towards him. It was impossible to determine whether he would stand a better chance of winning the girl's complaisance (if that was what he sought) by abandoning his attempt to interest her in the moth, perhaps by letting it fly away, and concentrating on less indirect attempts at persuasion, such as stroking her tawny hair and paying her compliments, or by continuing to exhibit the captive moth, offering at the same time a sort of lecture on natural history which might win the girl's confidence and be turned later to good effect as it led to more intimate conversation.

The situation was possibly as challenging for the shepherd to resolve as it was for the onlooker. If the girl was married to the shepherd's employer, the situation might be even more difficult. For it was possible that under her heavy lids she was looking at him in a way which he was at liberty to misinterpret as encouraging; he might then run his hands through that tawny hair, so soft about the nape of the neck; he might even attempt —half succeed!—to kiss that plump underlip; and she might then go to her husband and reveal what had taken place, thus involving the shepherd in a number of troubles; or, once in that difficult position, he might be unsure whether it had been brought about because the girl had told her husband voluntarily, or whether, in his plodding way, the husband had forced a confession from her. He might be dismissed from his post, to hover for ever after like a troubled spirit about the scene and cause of the disaster.

'This is another discussion of the painting of Holman Hunt's!' exclaimed the Suppressor of the Archives, who was acting as the senior juryman of the ten.

He walked softly across the darkened room and laid his hand on the shoulder of the tranced woman, who immediately ceased to deliver her report. As her singsong voice died, the jurymen seemed to come alive. One of them, whose official role was Impaler of Distortions, touched his lamp and said, 'Since, it seems to me, this Holman Hunt painting has fully as much substance as the world in which the Wandering Virgin now finds her-self, I took the liberty to have my servant Imago bring us a facsimile of the work in question. Here it is now. Imago!'

A man in ragged velvet advanced from the rear of the court bearing a large canvas, which he held before each of the jurymen in turn. The jurymen scrutinized it with varying degrees of absorption.

'As you will observe,' said the Impaler, 'the Wandering Virgin has given us what in some respects we must regard as an accurate report on this minor and totally negligible work of art, though I myself would have placed more emphasis on the banal symbolism of the painting—that, for instance, the young shepherd carries a ram's horn slung over one shoulder, possibly denoting cuckoldry, or that the girl is nursing, not only green apples, but a cloth-bound volume entitled "Low Point X", which may be taken as a reference to her mental state, or that—'

The jurymen knew the length of the Impaler's speeches. The Impersonator of Sorrows, interrupting, said, 'While agreeing that it is certainly a coincidence that this . . . er, universe that the Virgin describes should contain a painting which clearly belongs in our own universe—a fairly well-known painting by a minor Island English artist—I am surprised, Impaler, that you should therefore assume that this universe has the same degree of actuality as the painting. We know the painting exists, but do we know the universe exists? No! Quite clearly, the Virgin is describing some inner world of her own, which cannot be regarded as real or actual just because it contains external referents.'

'How then do you account for Domoladossa and this

fellow Growleth, Master Impersonator?' enquired the Sup-pressor.

'Why sir, how, sir? By understanding that they are merely additional bulwarks of the dear Virgin's imagin-ings: and clearly if we are to leave here alive, we must decide that they are merely imaginings and the "world" containing G and S and the rest mere fancy.'

The Image Motivator waved the painting aside and said, with a trace of impatience, 'Let us not be too sophis-ticated, lest we miss the point. The Wandering Virgin has provided us with facts in her report on this universe which she could not have known in her own right. I will give you an instance.

'Happily, the Impaler of Distortions is not the only dilettante in the arts. I have long known this canvas of the Hireling Shepherd and—unlike our friend apparently —rate it very highly in the social history of oil-painting. It embodies all the preoccupations of the Victorian Age, such as their attitude towards nature and the promptings of morality. It also embodies—demonstrates, perhaps I should say—their painful incarceration within time, with which they were unable to come to terms even upon a theoretical level. So their painters became masters of the Unresolved, of the What Next? instant: the dilemma, the unanswered question, the suspended gesture, the pause before destruction—or, on the other hand, the hour of disaster, nemesis, prompting a glance back at previous moments. Almost all the greatest Victorian pictures repre-sent the imprisonment of beings in a temporal structure that seemed at the time to admit of no escape; so the paintings are cathartic in essence.

'The Hireling Shepherd, in company with other master-

125

*pieces of its period, is, in the last analysis, a psychody-
namic drama of unresolved time, although executed in
representational mode, as was then the fashion. And, incidentally, that S also sees it this way is confirmed by his
identifying his own situation with the one depicted by
Hunt.*

*'Now, the Wandering Virgin's report hints at just this
understanding of Victorian painting, which I suggest is
knowledge that does not normally belong to our fair
traveller. Therefore, the report is being beamed to her by
some entity, possibly Mr. Mary himself—or his wife, for
in some ways she seems to be the crucial character—who
actually lives in the universe reported on. Which is proof
sufficient that it exists, gentlemen.'*

*'That's all nonsense!' said the Impersonator, but the
Squire of Reason said, 'I like the Motivator's logic, sirs.
I go along with that. Time is of the essence here. Is not
the whole report an account of the failure of time in that
particular universe, the Marian Universe, as we might
conveniently term it, just as we are threatened with a
temporaneous collapse here? Is it not a fact that these
people we hear about are rendered immobile, powerless
—no doubt by a time-failure? Suppressor, pray induce our
wandering lady to proceed!'*

The white below the picture was flecked with brown
spots. The floor below the picture was uneven. The shoes
were dusty. The trousers were dusty. S banged at the
trousers with his right hand.

Bowing his shoulders, he moved under the cross-beam
towards a long arrangement of shelves and partitions

that stood against the wall behind the hammock. On and in these shelves was a collection of articles belonging to or acquired by S, including three empty jam jars and a jar containing runner bean seeds; a bowler hat, in the rim of which lay a patent inhaler designed to fit up a nostril; a worm-eaten leg of an upright chair; a tartan plastic fountain pen; a perished hot water bottle; a brass handle off a drawer; a cotton reel containing brown thread; an empty pigskin purse; a china candlestick of an earlier age, on which was printed a representation of a devil breathing fire; a paperbound book entitled 'Low Point X', the cover of which curled upwards, exposing brown pages; a broken coach lantern lying cheek-by-jowl with a group of three walnuts; a straw hat of the kind called 'boater', bound round by a red and blue ribbon; an umbrella with a handle representing a fox's head lying under the boater; two enamel notices bearing the legend Beware of the Dog in black letters; a small collection of groceries and eating utensils, including a cracked blue and white cup and an unopened tin of sardines; a small brass crocodile; a bundle of newspaper; an enamel chamber pot with no handle; some shaving things lying in a small basin with floral decorations on it; a brass hinge and an iron key; an ancient tennis ball with most of its knap missing; a brief-case; the skeleton of a long-eared bat with its left ear missing; a pottery cart-horse with its head missing; and a mousetrap still bearing a crumb of cheese on its single rusty tooth. Most of these articles were covered with a fine dust. S picked up the bundle of newspaper that lay next to the brass crocodile and climbed with it into the hammock.

Over his body he arranged two grey woollen blankets

and a sort of rug made out of sacks stuffed with newspaper. Opening the newspaper, he lifted from it half of a pork pie, which had been cut through the middle, so that half of a hard-boiled egg was revealed, yellow and white, embalmed in the middle of the meat. S held it in his right hand, biting into it, while with his left hand he smoothed out the newspaper against the sack covering his left leg.

When he had smoothed the newspaper sufficiently, he brought it up so that it caught the light from the round window. He was regarding a page filled with reviews of books. He began to read the first review at the top of the left-hand column; it dealt with a volume entitled 'The Ethics of Language', and commenced with the sentence: With a seeming inevitability, every branch of knowledge develops its own specialized concepts. After he had stuffed the last chunk of pie into his mouth, S wiped his hands on the paper and dropped it onto the floor.

He adjusted a dismembered bear more comfortably under his head and lay back on the hammock, his eyes gazing up at the tiles visible between the beams overhead. Occasionally he blinked his eyes.

'Are you in there, because I'm going home now?'

S sat up. He looked to the right side and to the left side. He slid out of the hammock and went to the window, crouching to the left of it and peering to the right. Outside, it was dull, and the sky was thick with cloud. His gaze met a dirt path, running parallel with an asparagus bed, with a stretch of lawn behind it. A plump woman stood on the dirt path, dressed in a voluminous kidney-coloured coat, and wearing on her head a hat on which artificial flowers gleamed. She carried a basket in her left hand. With her right hand she beckoned up at S.

'I said I'm off home now. I've got my own work to do, you know, unlike some people. Here's your lamp been standing here. Come and take it in before it starts to rain.'

'Where are they?'

'Never mind about them. I've done the washing up and they're in the sitting-room over coffee. It's going to pour with rain before I get home, I shouldn't wonder.'

'Has he got his gun?'

'You talk so silly. Are you coming down to get this lamp? I filled it for you this morning.'

'Thank you very much.'

'Well, are you coming down or aren't you?'

'Why didn't you put it beside the little door?'

'Look, if he found I was pinching his paraffin, there'd be trouble. *You* know what Mr. Mary is. Are you coming down before I go?'

'I'll come down presently. I was having a sleep.'

'Having a sleep! Did you enjoy the pie? I'm off. I've got work of my own. I haven't got all day. It's coming on to rain.'

'I'll be down presently.'

'I'm off then. I'll see you tomorrow, I suppose.'

'Vi—he saw me this morning.'

'It is his garden, you know. Cheerio, then.'

She turned her back on the old brick building and began walking up the dirt path beside the asparagus bed, carrying her basket in her left hand.

When she reached the lawn at the back of the house,

she turned right and went across to a garage built mainly of asbestos sheets and concrete pillars. In the back of this garage was a door, which she opened. She went into the garage.

6

At the back of the garage, there was a square hole in the ceiling where a ladder bolted to the wall gave access to the roof space. The plump woman directed her gaze up towards this space.

'Just going to pick up my umbrella and I'm off. Here's a bit of cake for you.'

'Don't know what I'd do without you, that's a fact.'

'Well, come and get it then, or shall I leave it on the bench here? Ooh, you men, you don't half want looking after.'

'You're always in such a hurry, Violet. I'm coming down.'

'I've got work of my own. It's coming on to rain by the looks of things. I've just remembered I've forgotten my umbrella. I'll forget my own head one of these days.'

'How'd you forget a thing that size? Where's the cake?'

A man in stockinged feet climbed down the upright ladder that was bolted to the rear wall of the concrete and asbestos garage. He was small and hard. He grinned at the plump woman. He continued to grin till her face responded.

'Where's this bit of cake you brought me, then, Violet? Hand it over. I can't stand here all day. Some of us have work to do.'

'Yes, and I don't want any of your lip! It's only a small slice, so that they wouldn't miss it.'

'He wouldn't come in here looking for it if he did miss it.'

'Don't you be so cocky. You men'll try him too far one of these days. George will wonder where I've got to, standing here.'

'And what about her?'

'What about her?'

'Don't give me that. Did she talk about me this morning?'

'I don't tell tales, so it's no good trying to get round me. She'll be going out to see her friend in half an hour, if you must know.'

'I'll drive her there.'

'Oh shut up! You make me sick, all three of you. I'm going.'

'I would. I'd drive her there. I often get in the car and pretend to be driving. It helps pass the time. Here we go, I say. Where you will, Madam Jeanette. Just passing through Windsor, Guildford, Hindhead, Arundel, Chichester. Lovely day for a drive. Is madam comfortable?'

'Honest, I think you're mad.'

'Jump in. I'll give you a ride. You're always in such a hurry.'

'I've got some shopping to do before I get home. George will be wondering where I am. I must remember to pick up that umbrella as I go. A chap like you, pretending to drive a car! I'd better get on before it rains.'

'See you tomorrow, then. Thanks for the cake.'

'Why don't you get out of here before something terrible happens?'

'See you tomorrow, Violet.'

Against the rear wall of the garage, an upright ladder had been bolted. Clutching his slice of cake in one hand, C climbed lightly up the ladder and through a square hole in the ceiling. He emerged in a narrow storage space under the roof.

The Governor, Domoladossa, and Midlakemela stared at each other in surprise.

'It's an extraordinary situation,' the latter said. 'I'd say this probability world, if that is what it is, is several degrees from ours. Even the names of the places we've been given are entirely foreign.'

'And their behavior!' said the Governor. 'Let's get this clear. Here's the house. There's a café opposite, where apparently nobody pays for food. In the grounds of the house, there's a wooden summerhouse on one side, an old stable at the back, and a garage on the other side. We know there's an ex-gardener camping out more or less permanently in the summerhouse, and an ex-secretary camping out in the old stable. Now we're given to under-

stand there's an ex-chauffeur hiding out over the garage!
Quite unbelievable!'

'Unbelievable, yes,' Domoladossa said. 'And yet curiously credible. If only we could glimpse their motives.
. . . You notice all three of the watchers seem to take
interest in Mrs. Mary. I still say she's the key to the
whole thing.'

'It's all oddly innocent,' Midlakemela said.

'I find it all damned SINISTER,' the Governor said.

'Oh well, I must go for lunch,' Domoladossa said. 'I'm
late already, and it's veal today.'

Part Three

The House and The Watchers

Joe Growleth got back from lunch refreshed. He had come to a firm conclusion: their robot fly had not penetrated another dimension or anything like that. It had entered into some weird kind of mental communication.

This conclusion was eminently satisfying to Joe. The math behind the actuality of the fly was complex, and it could be that here at last was the desired bridge between the mental and the physical. He went back cheerfully into the stale room and looked up at the big screen.

Charlock and Corless were strolling back up the hillside from the lodge. Both wore raincoats, for cloud was closing in and a light drizzle had started. They were smiling and obviously in complete accord.

'We're agreed then,' Charlock said. 'We have here a

local flaw in the structure of the universe. It must clearly be infinitesimal, otherwise the world would be disrupted. So, through this freak, we are permitted to see into a sub-atomic world—and find it startlingly like our own!'

'Just a question of scale,' Corless said. 'And who knows if we ourselves. . . .' He paused. Some thoughts were too tremendous for utterance.

The two men halted before the apparition in the air. They looked through the framed photograph on the desk in time to see Domoladossa returning cheerfully from lunch.

Domoladossa had come to a conclusion over lunch. Probability World A held the clue to other probabilities beyond that. Once they had solved the riddle of its nature, it might be possible to visit there in person. He sat down and took up the report, curious to find what C was doing, lurking above the garage.

Even in the centre of the loft, under the highest line of roof, it was too low for C to walk entirely upright. He hunched his shoulders and proceeded to the front of the loft, where a small window had been set into the sheet of asbestos. The window was square, with sides measuring half a metre. Two crossed bars divided it into four square panes. Three of these panes were covered with dirt on the outside. The lower left-hand pane had been broken and entirely removed. The window was not designed to open. The sill of the window was about two thirds of a metre above the floor; C went and squatted by the window, in such a way that his eyes looked over the edge of the sill and through the window.

In his right hand he held a slice of cake from which he took large bites.

He stared through the window at a road. The road ran south-east. On the other side of it was a wide pavement; a tall man wearing black overalls and a grey felt hat passed along the pavement, followed at some distance by two men in blue carrying a stretcher on which lay a bicycle with two flat tyres; the frame of the bicycle was covered with blood. The surface of the road was of a dark crumbling texture. Cars passed along it, four of them bearing black crêpe ribbons tied to their radiators.

The road was bounded chiefly by high brick walls, generally surmounted by pieces of broken bottle embedded in concrete, or by railings sharply pointed, so that they stood like spears pointing towards the clouds. Here and there was a greenhouse at which flowers could be bought, or a private brewery, or a clinic at which the poor people might have their pets killed free of charge, or a café. A café stood almost opposite the unopenable window of the garage.

This café had two long shop windows, one on either side of a recessed door. Outside the café were stands bearing various vegetables, oranges, bales of material, and newspapers. Over the café was a board bearing the words 'Stationer Family G. F. WATT Grocer Café Snacks Draper.' Through the window could be seen a variety of goods. G. F. Watt could also be seen, standing inside one of the windows with his arms folded, looking out across the road.

C stuffed the last piece of the slice of cake into his mouth and rubbed the fingers of the right hand against the fingers of the left hand.

'She's not so bad, old Violet.'

Lying below the window on the floor of the loft was a home-made instrument. It was constructed of six cylindrical tins each some ten centimetres high. The top of each tin had been pushed into the tin above it to form a tube some forty-four metres long. In the bottom and the top tin, holes had been created, so that small tabs of metal pointed inwards, holding in place two mirrors, one at the top and one at the bottom of the tube. These pieces of mirror were set at angles of forty-five degrees to the axis of the tube. In the sides of the top and bottom tins facing the two mirrors, circular openings had been cut. Anyone looking into the bottom of these circular openings could see reflected in the bottom mirror whatever was reflected in the top mirror. The instrument was a home-made periscope.

C picked up the home-made periscope and thrust one end through the bottom left-hand corner of the window. He sat on the left side of the window, with his stockinged right foot under his buttocks. He revolved the tin bottom section of his periscope in one direction while, with his other hand, revolving the rest of the periscope tube in an opposite direction. At a certain point, he stopped this motion, and stared into the small mirror set in the bottom of the tube. Through it, he could see the reflection in the top mirror of a small stretch of street otherwise inaccessible to his eyesight.

The arrangement of mirrors showed the east corner of the house, the side nearest to the asbestos garage, where it was joined by a wall facing the street. In the corner where the top of the wall, capped by rounded cement in which pieces of broken glass had been embedded, met the bricks of the house, a tuft of grass grew. Taking in this tuft of grass, the arrangement of mirrors moved slightly, so that it gave C an oblique view of the front of the house and of the wall beyond the house.

So oblique was this view that it needed long study before it could be interpreted.

Seen from this angle and through an arrangement of mirrors that permitted a glimpse of only part of it at once, the front of the house was distorted into a thin diamond shape, the only features of it immediately distinguishable being a curved stone porch supported by two stone pillars, and a pair of stone steps, on the two ends of which rested the bases of the pillars.

Aslant from this porch ran the pavement that passed the house. As the watcher watched, a man passed along the pavement, carrying a deflated inner tube of a bicycle tyre in his bare hands. The arrangement of mirrors did not swing to follow him, so that his feet and legs were first visible, then the rest of his body and his face, the eyebrows of which had been removed, as he came level with the front door; his feet and legs began to disappear into the foreground of the reflection almost at once; soon most of the bicycle tube had also gone, but there then seemed to be an interval when the man walked for some paces before the upper part of his body dropped below the range of the periscope.

When the man carrying the bicycle tube had gone, the pavement remained empty.

On one point along the steep perspective of brick visible in the arrangement of mirrors was the appearance of a niche which, to a skilled observer, could be interpreted as the position of a brown side gate set in the wall on the far side of the house. From this niche appeared the point of a rolled umbrella, followed immediately by a rolled umbrella and a plump woman wearing a kidney-coloured coat and a small hat and carrying a basket. Her image, distorted by a flaw in one of the mirrors, represented her as a tall thin woman.

She turned to face in a south-easterly direction and walked in that direction along the pavement, so that she was inadvertently approaching the periscope. The periscope moved to keep her in range as well as it could.

The thin-looking plump woman turned her eyes towards the opposite side of the road where stood a café. She slightly raised her umbrella, as if in response to a salutation from that direction.

'What would George say if he could see you carrying on with old Watt? He'd lock you up, that's what he'd do, my ducks!'

In the arrangement of mirrors, the woman became curiously foreshortened as she drew nearer. Her legs disappeared, and with them all but the moving toes of the ankle boots in which her feet were enclosed. At the same time, her bosom and stomach took on undue prominence.

As she progressed, the image of her face became eclipsed by forehead, hair, and hat, on which drooped imitation flowers, nodding like pink, blue, and yellow snowdrops. Behind her head a knot of hair worked into a bun became visible. As she moved, so C moved the longer section of the periscope to keep her in sight.

The top of the head with its small hat was large now. The yellowy white hair combed into the bun was visible. The back of the liver-coloured coat became visible, more and more, until heels and then stockinged legs were also noticeable under it. Now the whole length of the plump woman was contained in the arrangement of mirrors; she was retreating down the road, carrying an umbrella in one hand and a shopping basket in the other. The right half of her body was distorted by a flaw in the glass. Over her shoulder as she became smaller with distance could be glimpsed a distant white cross with, beyond it, a row of columns that ran along the façade of the railway station.

'You see, it's not going to rain, for all your worrying.'

The periscope was withdrawn from the bottom left-hand corner of the small window. It was placed below the window.

C turned away from the window and sat with his back to it. He set his stockinged feet in front of his buttocks so that his knees were almost on a level with his face; he rested his arms on top of the knees and his chin on top of the arms.

The distance between him and the square window at the back of the garage, which looked over the garden of the house, was not more than five and a half metres. To his left, this distance was occupied by a sharp-prowed canoe painted a light blue. The name Flier was painted in white letters on the side of the canoe. Rests made of a light wood supported the canoe in an upright position. Inside the canoe, the seats had been removed and the space was filled with a mixture of wood shavings and blankets covered by a small tarpaulin. The tarpaulin was black; small cracks ran all over it. One end of the tarpaulin was draped over the far side of the canoe, where two paddles lay in dust. The dust was thick. It became less thick in the centre of the floor, but gathered again on the other side. The floor was made of narrow planks, and divided into two slightly differing parts. The first two metres of floor ran from under the front window to a crack across the width of the loft. Beyond this crack, the rest of the planks to the back of the garage were removable in joined groups of four, so that this end of the floor could be temporarily removed to transfer any large objects such as canoes from the body of the garage to the loft.

Along the other side of the loft, the right side as C sat, lay a series of cardboard boxes bearing the names of various products, soap, cornflakes, and baked beans, and containing C's possessions. Against one of the boxes lay a pair of boots. They were black; they had recently been polished until they shone. They contrasted with the dirty and darned socks on C's feet.

The cardboard boxes were closed. On top of the one nearest the front of the garage lay a square paper book with a bright cover. The title of the paper book was 'City Murder Chillers'. The cover depicted a man trapped on a wooden plank between two skyscrapers. In each hand he held a gun. He was firing at four men who seemed to be running towards him. Behind him, another man with a blowlamp was attempting to burn through the wooden plank. C picked up the paper book and opened it. It consisted chiefly of coloured picture stories. The first story was called Among the Missing. C began to look at it.

When he had turned two pages, he shut the book, tossing it to a corner of the loft with a flip of his wrist. The book landed in the dusty wedge of space where the roof sloped down and met the floor. The roof was made of a light metal, bent into a regular pattern to strengthen it. It had come in sheets; at regular intervals, several rows of bolts ran from one end of the garage to the other, clamping these sheets together. The ends of most of these bolts were green.

In the loft, the light was dim. A slight noise began to fill the loft. It grew in volume. As rain fell from the sky, it landed on the sloping roof of the garage. The sloping roof was of light metal. The rain drummed on it. As the rain came down more heavily, the noise increased in volume. The rain ran down the two sides of the roof into rain gutters that edged the roof. The gutters fed into two vertical drainpipes set one on either side of the garage. The water bubbled into the drainpipes with a noise that could be heard inside the loft. No rain came inside the loft.

'The old girl was right, after all!'

Getting to his feet, C hunched his shoulders and moved to the window at the back of the garage. The window had not been designed to open. It was small and square, with two bars of wood dividing it into four squares. Three of the squares were glazed. The bottom right-hand square had had its glass removed. Rain came in the hole. In the dirt just below the window was a block of wood, thick, and shaped to fit into the bottom right-hand square of the window. C picked it up and wedged it into place in the hole. The rain stopped coming through the hole.

C looked out of the window.

'Quite a nice little shower!'

The view through the three panes of glass in the window was distorted by rain pouring down the glass. To the thickness of the glass were added the convolutions of water, flowing irregularly downwards, spreading over the glass. The patterns the water made as it ran down the glass were always changing.

The view of the garden encompassed on the left a high brick wall, the top of which was capped by rounded concrete blocks; in the cracks between the blocks small green ferns grew. This wall was the wall bounding Mr. Mary's estate on its south-east side. It ran straight down the boundary, dividing the garden from the yard of a banana importer and distributor, until at its far end it met a privet hedge dividing the garden from a garden belonging to an unmarried man known to have a grandfather who had built a lighthouse somewhere along the coast of Africa or South America. The point at which the brick wall and the privet hedge met (the southern corner of the garden) was concealed from the window in the garage by a cluster of shrubs that fringed an ornamental pool. The cluster of shrubs was obscured by the water running down the window.

More distantly, and now distorted by the rain pouring down the window of the garage, the hedge could be seen bounding the longest side of the long lawn. On the other side of it lay a dirt path upon which puddles now gathered. Both privet hedge and dirt path ran down to an old brick building that had once served as a coach house.

The coach house, though its outlines trembled and were uncertain because of the rain now coursing over the small window of the garage, was easily visible to C. When he had first taken refuge in the loft of the garage, six months ago, the old brick building had been almost entirely hidden behind the summer foliage of the apple and plum and pear trees. Only its tiled roof had been visible. The tiled roof was visible now.

'He must be getting a regular shower bath in there. You can't tell me that roof would keep the rain out for long. Bet it's pouring down on him!'

The front of the coach house could be seen through the rain. In the upper half of it, a round window was set in the brickwork. At this distance, in this light, no detail could be discerned. Below the round window, two large doors ran across the façade of the building. The doors were dark with wet.

'Better him than me.'

A pigeon known as X clattered from a point in the brickwork somewhere above the round window, circled awkwardly with its wing-tips appearing to clap together first above then below the tip of its body, and flew northwards behind the bulk of the house. Rain fell. It poured over the windows of the garage and obscured the view.

From time to time, Domoladossa interrupted his reading of the report to make a sketch map on a rough pad which lay on his desk near the framed photograph of his wife. Following the information given in the report, he now carefully drew in a few more details.

'It's a human problem, of course,' he muttered. He determined to volunteer to be the first to enter this probability world; he would go straight to Mrs. Mary—when they had more information on her.

2

On the roof of the garage rain fell. The roof, constructed
with a light metal, gave off a resonant noise under the
continued impact of thousands of drops of rain. The roof
did not leak. At regular intervals along the inside of the
roof ran several rows of bolts, secured in place with nuts.
These bolts kept in place the sheets of metal that together comprised the roofing. Most of these nut and bolt
combinations were green; the others were grey, their original colour. The green ones began to glisten. The ends
of them began to glisten. Whether one looked at them or
looked away, the glistening ends swelled slowly.

On the glistening ends of the bolts, drops of water
formed. The bolt ends that were grey did not have glistening ends. Along the inside of the roof, six rows of

bolt ends began to glisten. The light from the unopening window at the front of the asbestos garage was caught by a series of small raindrops hanging from the roof. The drops imprisoned and reflected the light. One by one the drops fell to the planks on the loft floor.

'It looks as if it's never stinking well going to stop. God, how I'd like—oh, it's all the same!'

The drops did not fall in unison. Water collected on each bolt at a different rate. Each glistening end kept its own tempo. Some of the bolts seemed as if they would remain dry once their current drip had been shed; but slowly a point of moisture grew, containing a highlight within it. And the point of moisture extended itself into a droplet. With the slowest bolts, the droplets would hang there for a time to be measured in minutes; eventually the droplet would extend itself, stretch towards the floor, part company with the end of the bolt, and strike off on its own for the floor.

Despite the noise made by the rain as it drummed on the light metal roof, C could hear the drops inside as they struck the floor.

The rate at which the various bolts secreted water could be judged by looking at the floor. Under a slow bolt would be merely a dark patch of wetness extending along the grain of the plank. Under a faster bolt, a small puddle would collect. The small puddles had untidy edges, for when the next drop fell into them, a miniature tidal wave was created. As more puddles appeared, most of them only a couple of centimetres across, the noise of the drops striking the floor changed in character. From a dull heavy note, it now took on a livelier and more liquid sound.

Moving on his hands and toes, with his knees only a little way off the floor, C scuttled to the other end of the garage. By going down the centre of the loft, it was simple to avoid the small puddles.

He put his back to the front wall of the garage and sat down on the floor beside the square window. Pulling his knees up so that they were on a level with his shoulders, he rested his arms across his knees and his chin on his hands. He gazed ahead of him. He whistled a tune called Whistling Rufus.

Along the side of the loft nearest to the house, the right side as C sat, a series of large cardboard cartons had been aligned. They contained C's possessions. On the outside of them were the names of the goods they had once contained, baked beans, soap, and cornflakes. There were five of the cartons. They stood in positions on the floor where the drips from the bolts in the roof did not strike them. The small puddles collected behind them, where the roof ran very close to the floor of the loft, and in front of them, but did not touch the boxes.

On the other side of the loft lay a canoe with a sharp prow. It was built of wood and rested on wooden rests that kept it steadily upright. The outside of the hull had been painted a light blue. The name of the boat, Flier, was painted on its prow in white paint. The canoe occupied almost all the space between front and back of the loft.

Because the canoe was narrow, it had been possible to arrange that it stood in such a position that none of the drips from the bolts on the roof fell on it, except amidships, where the boat was widest. At this point, drips from two bolts fell on it. The contents of the canoe were mainly blankets and wood shavings, but a tarpaulin saved them from a wetting. The tarpaulin lay across the canoe with one end hanging over the edge, towards the floor. The drips from the two bolts overhead collected on this tarpaulin and rolled off onto the floor.

C stopped whistling. Lifting his chin, he raised his right hand and scratched the back of his head. He replaced his hand on his knee and replaced his chin on the hand. He tapped on the floor with one stockinged foot and began to whistle again. He whistled a tune called Whistling Rufus.

Ahead and to the right of where he sat stood five cardboard boxes. They contained C's possessions. Small puddles collected in front of these boxes (and behind, where they were unseen by C). The puddles encroached on the dust of the floor; sometimes small pieces of fluff sailed on them. The puddles were not all of the same size. Some were bigger than others. The bigger ones were larger than the smaller ones. The smaller ones were not as large as the medium-sized ones. The larger ones gathered under the bolts that collected drips most quickly. The smaller ones gathered under the bolts that collected drips less quickly. The bolts were bolted on the roof. The puddles lay on the floor. The puddles wetted the floor. The floor was wetted by the puddles lying on it.

C closed his eyes and stopped whistling.

He reopened his eyes and shook his head slowly to and fro. He opened his mouth and yawned. He blinked his eyes.

At the far end of the loft was a small square window divided into four panes. The bottom left pane had been blocked by a square of wood. Over the remaining three panes, water trickled, distorting the view. From where C sat, he could see only a distorted piece of brick wall to the left; the rest was a blur of greens, browns, and greys.

On his right as he sat, running down the right-hand side of the loft, were five brown cardboard boxes. They were flanked by puddles. Many forces of nature, including thermal and gravitational effects, had created the dirty little puddles on the floor.

From the roof, six rows of bolt ends protruded into the loft. Most of them gleamed.

Getting onto his knees, C crawled down the length of the loft until he reached the last cardboard box. It bore a legend that showed it had originally contained baked beans. C stood up with bent shoulders and opened the top of the box. He reached down and rummaged into it. As he did so, he could see some squares of wood resting behind the box.

From the box, he pulled a stiff cap with a shining peak. Holding it in his left hand, he rubbed the peak with his right sleeve. The peaked cap had been given to him when he entered Mr. Mary's service thirteen months ago. He put it onto his head. He pushed his hair back under the cap. He smiled. He straightened his back slightly and saluted, touching the peak with the stiff fingers of his right hand.

'Reporting for duty, sir. All ready to go. Everything in order, sir.'

Dropping his arm, he turned to the hole in the floor that lay to the side of the loft nearest the house. Through the hole protruded the top of a ladder, bolted upright to the rear side of the garage. C reached out to the ladder and climbed down it. He stood on the floor of the garage.

In the garage, the light was dim. Some illumination filtered down through the trap to the loft from the square window set in the back wall. Set in the north-west side of the garage was a small window hinged at the top and set high in the wall. It looked onto the side of the house. Since a space of no more than one and a half metres separated garage and house, the small window gave little light. At the front of the garage, the double doors each contained windows of a reinforced glass through which it was impossible to see, although light was conducted through it into the garage.

Occupying most of the floor of the garage was a black car of British manufacture. Although its body was painted with enamel, which threw up long highlights here and there, it seemed to absorb rather than reflect light. The four tyres of the car were flat; it rested on the rims of the wheels.

'The report goes into too much detail!' Midlakemela said. He had been reading over Domoladossa's shoulder.

Domoladossa did not reply. The report conveyed to him completely the boredom of C's vigil above the garage, the man's obsessive and unrecognizing gaze across the objects about him. Now they—Domoladossa and Midlakemela—were subjecting those objects to a second scrutiny. They were having to determine WHAT WAS OF VALUE; *until that was decided, this life was valueless. Find significance and all is found.*

Of course, Domoladossa was unaware that he was being scrutinized by the Distinguishers on their rainy hillside. They, in their turn, were being watched by the grave men in New York. They, in their turn, were being watched

by two young men and a boy who stood in an empty
warehouse staring at the manifestation in puzzlement.
'What is it, Daddy?' asked the boy.

'We've discovered a time machine or something,' the
father said. He leaned farther forward; it was just possible
to make out Domoladossa reading his report, for the New
York screen showed the hillside manifestation revealing
him at his desk.

Apart from the car and the windows, the features of
the garage were few. The double doors in the front were
secured by a patent tumbler lock and by long black bolts
top and bottom. Near one of the double doors, the door
with its hinges on the side of the garage nearest to the
house, was a wooden fuse box. From this fuse box, wire
encased in black rubber led up to a switch at shoulder
height. A further length of wire encased in black rubber
led from the switch to a light fitting above the car in
which hung a naked light bulb.

The rear wall of the garage had three features. On the
side nearest to the house was a door that led into the
garden. It was shut now. It was a light metal door. It
had a handle on the inside; on the outside were handle
and key. Across the light metal panel in the top of the
door had been scrawled in black paint the symbol 12A.
Next to the door was a ladder made of white wood. It was
bolted against the concrete supports of the garage, thus
remaining upright and leading up into the loft. Beyond
the ladder, and occupying most of the rest of the rear
wall of the garage, was a carpenter's bench equipped with
a vice and with a sawing trestle standing underneath it.

On top of the bench, near the ladder, stood a dull red oil drum with a tap at the bottom of it. Beneath the tap on the concrete floor of the garage stood a drip tray and a metal funnel. Some paraffin lay in the drip tray. The rest of the top of the bench was littered with tools relating to the car or to carpentry, with coils of wire and flex and grimy rags lying on tops of the tools.

In the wall facing the house, the only feature was a small window opening outwards with its hinges at the top. The wall opposite consisted of asbestos sheets interspersed with reinforced concrete pillars; it was otherwise featureless.

Brushing along this featureless wall, C opened the driver's door of the car and climbed in. The leather upholstery of the seating was grey. C settled himself in the driver's seat, leant forward to grasp the handle of the door, and pulled the door shut.

The windows of the car were all closed. Inside the car, it was less easy to hear the rain falling on the garage. An occasional but regular tap on the roof of the car signified to C that water from small puddles on the floor of the loft above the car was leaking through and down onto the car.

'And where would you care to go on this lovely sunny day, madam? Speak up, madam. Distance no object. Would madam care to try Brighton for a paddle?'

Grimacing, C pretended to switch on the ignition. He pulled the starter. He put a stockinged foot on the accelerator. He pressed gently on the accelerator. Pressing the clutch down, he eased the gear lever into first gear. He held the steering wheel with both hands, turning it gently.

He removed his left hand and changed into second gear. He smiled and nodded into the back seat.

'Has madam made up madam's pretty little mind yet? Distance no object, madam. Torquay? Virginia Water? How about Henley-on-Thames or the Lake District? Should be lovely round Windermere on a lovely January day like this.'

C eased the car into third gear, and through into fourth almost immediately. He pressed his stockinged foot down on the accelerator. He held the steering wheel loosely in both hands, with his two thumbs on the outside of the wheel pointing outwards. He held his head high and looked keenly ahead at the closed double doors a few centimetres beyond the bonnet of the car.

'How's this, madam? Lovely day, eh? Aren't you glad we didn't bring that husband of yours? Perhaps madam would care for me to spread a rug on the ground when we stop, so that madam can lie herself down on the ground. Does madam realize how attractive she is in the prone position?'

His mouth opened wide, his eyebrows rose towards the line of his hair. Thrusting his head forward, he swung the wheel hard over to the right, at the same time letting his body slew to the right, until his right shoulder touched the driver's door. Slowly he came back into an upright position, gasping and wiping his forehead with the back of his left hand. He changed down into second gear and then back to fourth, finally allowing a smile to play over his features as he turned again to the back seat.

'Sorry about that, honey. I must keep my mind on my driving, madam. We nearly got that old girl, didn't we?

A couple of centimetres more round the waist and she'd have been a goner.'

Facing forward again, C ceased the pretence at driving. Resting both elbows through the steering wheel, he cupped his chin in his upthrust hands. He brought up his right leg, doubling it until the stockinged foot rested on the upholstery and the knee against the door of the car. His eyes still stared ahead.

He began to whistle a tune called Whistling Rufus. He changed his position, forgetting to whistle as he did so, arranging his legs across the passenger's seat so that he could rest his back against the door of the car and his right arm over the steering wheel. With the nails of the fingers of the right hand, he tapped against the steering wheel. With the left hand, he pushed his cap from behind so that it slid forward until the stiff peak rested along his nose. The left hand remained clamped at the back of the neck.

'Get out of this bloody set-up. You don't stand a chance. Get a job down on the coast somewhere, down in the sun. Go abroad. Go south. Nice little chauffeur's job on the Riviera. Drive a rich widow about. Get out of here.'

The fingers of his left hand began to tap against his neck. He drew up his left knee. Bringing his left hand away from the back of his neck, he rested it over the top of his left knee.

'Stuffy in here. Maybe stick it out a bit longer. At least you see her every day. Christ, what's life for, anyway?'

By ducking his head slightly, C could look through the small window with hinges in its upper side and see a small area on the south-east side of the house. A third of the visible area was brickwork; the rest was part of a narrow window of frosted glass. It was the upper part of a frosted glass window. By craning his neck further, he could see an overflow spout projecting from the brick wall beside the window. The window belonged to an upstairs lavatory. The view of it was obscured by the rain running down the pane of the garage window.

Sitting up again, C let his left leg slide down flat against the seat again, twisting his body to the left so that he could rest his arms over the back of the driver's seat. He rested his chin on top of his hands. Without interest, he gazed into the back seat. The darkness inside the car seemed particularly thick on the back seat.

'Don't let 'em get you down, boy. Bastards. All bastards, the lot of 'em. It's too late now anyway. You're swallowed like those snakes. Still, Monte Carlo, Nice—why not? Also among the missing. . . . Nobody'd care. Old Violet, perhaps.'

Raising his chin, C moved his right arm over to the back of the front seat, sliding it to and fro over the grey leather upholstery. With his left hand trapped under his chin, he began to tap with his left fingers on the upholstery beneath them. He whistled tunelessly, gazing down at the lines in the upholstery that ran from the front to the rear of the back seat.

'No point in hanging around here.'

C opened the car door and set foot on the garage floor. By the rear wheel of the car, a puddle had collected. Rainwater seeping through the bolt holes in the roof had dripped down the ends of the bolts onto the floor of the loft above the car; eventually small puddles had formed on the floor of the loft, some of which had dripped between the boards of the floor onto the roof of the car.

On either side of the roof of the car were small runnels into which the water dripping onto the top of the car had drained. The runnels followed the streamlining of the car and led down to a point just above the rear wing. The water from the top of the car had trickled over the rear wing and onto the concrete floor. It lay in a puddle against the grey skinny folds of the collapsed tyre.

C avoided the puddle as he went towards the ladder at the rear of the garage. He stood with his left hand resting on one of the rungs of the ladder, his right hand on his right hip, listening with his head cocked. He went forward and opened the light metal door that had the symbol 12A painted on its upper panel.

3

The rain had stopped.

From the earth came a constant fruity noise as the rainwater soaked away into the ground. In the sky above the sunken garden were a thinning of cloud and a suggestion of sky.

A length of grass bordered on its south-east side by a bed of standard rose bushes stretched down as far as a flight of four steps leading to a sunken garden. Just in front of the steps was a pigeon, pecking at the ground and thrusting its neck forward with every step it took.

At the back of the bed where the standard roses grew was a brick wall. It ran down the side of the garden, beyond the sunken garden, to meet a privet hedge at the bottom. On the other side of the sunken garden was an arrangement of banked flower beds, fringing the sunken garden with a long lawn on the other side of them. Growing from the long lawn were trees, their bare branches dripping. At the back of the trees, and partly screened by them, was a rubbish tip. Through the trees, lying more to the right, could be seen most of an old brick building. The lower part of the front of this old brick building was taken up by two sagging timber doors. Above the timber doors, set in the brickwork, was a round window. A slight movement could possibly be detected in the round window.

Raising his right hand, C folded it into a fist and shook it in the direction of the old brick building. He saw no more movement in the round window.

The south corner of the house cut off the larger and more northerly part of the garden from view. Several windows lay on the south-east side of the house overlooking the garage. C surveyed these windows. Their aspect was forbidding; they reflected only grey cloud. The overcast had not cleared, and the brief afternoon was yielding to sunset.

Next to the south corner of the house downstairs was a wide window. Through it, C could look into the diningroom. Part of a table was visible and, on the opposite wall, most of a sideboard on which stood some sort of a plant in a pot. On the wall above the sideboard could be seen a picture, the details of which were not clear. Clearly seen on the sill of the window was a china representation of a dog. The dog had large ears. It sat on its hind legs and tail and raised its forepaws in the air, begging. It faced into the room. The window was fringed on either side by green patterned curtains. Also visible through the window was the second of the dining-room's windows, this one set in the south-west wall of the house; not all of it could be seen from where C stood, because this was a long window, facing directly out onto the garden at the rear. The light from this window was reflected on the shining top of the dining-room table so clearly that the bars of the long window could also be seen in the reflection. By looking through both windows of the dining-room, C could observe a part of the garden not otherwise visible to him. Nothing could be clearly determined, except a few fruit trees and a privet hedge and, beyond the privet hedge, another property belonging to a bachelor whose grandfather had built a lighthouse somewhere along the coast of South Africa or South America.

On the first floor, a small bow window protruded some metres above the bricked recess. This bow window matched a similar one on the other side of the house, overlooking a wooden bungalow; this one was the window to Mr. Mary's wife's bedroom.

An expanse of brickwork followed, until a narrow window was reached. This window was glazed with frosted glass. It was built directly over a window in the ground floor that contained a similar section of frosted glass. It was the window of the upper lavatory. Beside it, a small overflow pipe stuck out from the face of the wall; a small overflow pipe stuck out of the wall beside the lower frosted window. Near the overflow pipes, a thick pipe ran down from the house into a square of concrete set in the ground.

Further along the wall was one more window, situated near the south corner of the house. It formed one of the two windows of the bathroom, the other window being round the corner on the south-west or rear side of the house. Through the window, blue curtains could be seen, and part of the shade of an electric light hanging from the ceiling. The colour of the shade could be seen to be blue. None of the other window could be seen from where C stood, although its presence was marked by a particular brightness across the bathroom ceiling emanating from the south-west. No movement was visible in the bathroom.

'She can't have gone out in all that rain.'

On the lawn, a pigeon waddled. A black and white cat stalked it, taking advantage of the cover of a privet hedge running from behind the house to the end of the foremost banked flower bed fringing the sunken garden. It moved to within a metre of the pigeon. It crouched, its skull pressed against its forepaws, its ears flat on its head. The pigeon moved away.

Through the window of the dining-room there was a movement. C turned his head and looked through the window. A woman with tawny hair swept up onto her head had entered the part of the room visible to C. She wore a light afternoon coat of brown tweed. She came round the table until she was between the window and the table, so that she was visible to C in profile. She was no more than two and a half metres from C, separated from him only by one thickness of glass. It appeared that she was about to look out of the long window that faced from the back of the house onto the garden. She stopped, and looked over her left shoulder. She looked at C.

C looked at the woman. Her lips were red. They had opened slightly. Neither C nor the woman moved. C raised his right hand in a gesture, at the same time slightly lowering his head, though still keeping her under observation.

The woman moved hastily out of sight. As she went it seemed to be that she contorted her face and opened her mouth. C moved into the garage and closed the door behind him.

He stood there, clutching the doorknob. Then he moved on his stockinged feet and climbed up a wooden ladder bolted to the rear wall of the garage. Near the top of the ladder in the loft was a small window that did not open. It was divided into four by two crossed bars. Three of these four sections were glazed; the bottom right section was not glazed. The glass had been removed, and in its place was a block of wood. C removed this block of wood. It was wet. He dropped it on the floor of the loft.

Just under the window lay a home-made periscope. It had been constructed from half a dozen round tins fitted one into the other to make a hollow tube some fifty-four metres long. Circular openings had been cut in the top and bottom tins facing onto two mirrors fitted into the tube at an angle of ninety degrees to each other. The bottom tin was made to rotate in its socket. Picking up this instrument, C prepared to push one end if it through the empty square of the window. As he did so, he glanced up and saw a movement in the dining-room window.

A man in dark suiting was looking round one of the green patterned curtains. His gaze was fixed on the window of the garage. In his right hand he carried a rifle, grasping it by the barrel.

C sank back into the shadows without removing his gaze from the man with the gun. The man did not move; only his eyes moved. C held the periscope. The man held the gun.

From the lawn came a shrill cry, and a clatter of noise. Both C and the man with the gun looked towards the lawn. Near to the point where the four steps descended into the sunken garden, a black and white cat had pounced upon and caught a large pigeon. The pigeon attempted to escape. It fluttered its wings and uttered a piercing cry. The cat was on its back. The fierce fluttering of wings startled the cat. It released the pigeon, which broke from it with a flurry of feathers. Running in a lop-sided manner, the pigeon beat its wings furiously. It left the ground. The cat sprang. Its paws raked the round body of the bird. With a more violent pulsation of its wings, the pigeon managed to remain in the air. Raising itself so that it danced on its hind legs, the cat clawed upwards, striking the pigeon even as it was struck on the nose by a battering wing. This frightened the cat. It dropped onto all fours in a manner that suggested that it might be about to retreat, but its dewclaw caught in a pewter ring that was fastened round one of the legs of the bird, so that the bird was dragged down on top of the cat. Frightened, the cat jumped round and pinned the pigeon to the ground with its paws. It put its mouth down to the pigeon's neck. The pigeon fluttered only feebly. Taking one of its wings into its mouth, the cat started to drag its victim over the grass. As it passed out of sight, obscured by the south corner of the house, the pigeon was still struggling.

The man with the gun moved away from the dining-room window. Still clutching his periscope, C went to the front of the garage, his shoulders hunched under the low roof, and sat with his back against the wall. He sat with his legs drawn up before him, his arms crossed over his knees, and his chin resting on his wrists. One end of the periscope rested against the side of his head.

'Get out of this bloody set-up. Go south. You don't stand a dog's chance here. Talk about snakes. . . .'

After a lapse of time, he placed the periscope by his right-hand side and moved crabwise to take in a view through the window.

No break showed in the clouds. Under a dull sky, the road showed dull. On the opposite side of the road could be seen railings with sharp spears pointing upwards and walls crowned with shards of broken bottles, guarding private property and the premises of small breweries, greenhouses, or vivisection clinics. Almost opposite the garage stood a café with lighted windows. The windows of the café were filled with all kinds of goods. Through one of the windows could be seen a small square table on which a red and white patterned cloth had been spread. Through the other window could be seen a man with folded arms, standing and looking across the road at the house.

C licked his lips. Turning his head away from the window, he leant sideways and picked up his home-made periscope. He thrust it through the hole in the bottom left corner of the window, adjusting it so that the top of the periscope was free of the top of the roof, and could look over it towards the south-east side of the house.

By peering along the line of his wrist, C could see in the bottom mirror of the periscope the reflection of what was visible in the top mirror. This gave him a limited but clear view into the small bow window that formed one of the two windows of Mr. Mary's wife's bedroom.

'My God, there she is! You're in luck. . . .'

Seated in the bow window, head bowed and fists clenched over her eyes, was the woman with tawny hair. She still wore the brown tweed coat. Her shoulders shook. Presently she removed one of her fists from her eyes to feel into a pocket concealed from C's line of sight. As it moved, the fist stretched into a long stalk of flesh, returning to its normal shape after it had passed over a flaw in one of the periscope mirrors. The flaw distorted the body of the woman, elongating and blurring her. Producing a small handkerchief, she mopped at her eyes and at her nose, while her shoulders continued to heave. A strand of her hair fell down across her neck. She was within about two and a half metres of the eye of the periscope.

'Huh, have a good weep! You might have been weeping for me instead of a miserable. . . . Hello! Here comes Smiling Boy!'

Behind the woman, a man in dark suiting appeared. He spoke to her. He placed a hand on her shoulder. She shook her shoulder away. He spread his hands. His lips could be seen opening and shutting. He smiled. Suddenly she turned her head towards him. She had high cheek-bones. The skin moved across the cheek-bones as her mouth opened and closed. The lips of both faces moved at once. The man was frowning now. Her cheeks were flushed. Her eyes were red; they could be seen as again he advanced towards her and again she turned away, trying to shake her shoulders from his clutch.

The man in dark suiting grasped her firmly now, although she struggled. He appeared to be shouting, although no sound reached C. The woman raised her fists, one of which clutched a handkerchief, above her head, and brought them down on her knees. Then she slumped forward with her forehead pressed against the window, making a white outline against it. Again her fists were raised to her eyes, and her eyes buried behind her knuckles, out of sight. The man in dark suiting shook his head and disappeared. The woman gave no indication that she knew he had gone from behind her.

C's arm was beginning to ache. He brought his regard away from the periscope mirror. Handling the instrument carefully, he pulled it in through the window; thrusting his right hand, which had been exposed, under his left armpit for warmth, he noted that it had grown appreciably duller outside. Only the fact that the woman with the tawny hair had been so close to the window had allowed him to see her clearly.

Pushing the peaked cap onto the back of his head, he stared out of the window. Street lights had come on while he was gazing through the periscope. The road looked drab. A motor hearse drove slowly down the street; above the cab, a neon sign flashed on and off forming a single word, Diggers. The hearse's tyres were deflating slowly. When the hearse had passed, a man began to cross the road towards the café opposite. He moved fast. C recognized him at once. It was the man in the dark suiting.

The man in the dark suiting crossed the road in a

certain number of strides. As he did so, the intensity of light falling on him varied greatly. When C first saw him, stepping from the pavement that was not visible from the inside of the garage window, his left shoulder was clearly illuminated by the light falling from a street light that C knew to be situated on the other side of the front of the house, between the house and a brown side gate in the wall beyond the house.

As the man in the dark suiting got further from this source, the street lighting tended to light the back of his left shoulder rather than the arm of it, growing fainter at the same time. A second street light, down the road in the opposite direction, beyond the east corner of the property, lit the man's suit with a pale illumination that served merely to distinguish the right side of his body from the dark of the street he was crossing. The lights from the windows of G. F. Watt's café lit the front of him increasingly, bathing his outline and the line of his jaw until, from C's viewpoint, the effect of the two more distant street lamps was nugatory.

As he entered the café door, the man was clearly visible under the lights. He walked into the café. The door hung open behind him. He walked to the counter, and the view of him was obscured by a pile of packaged goods arranged in the window.

Removing his right hand from his left armpit, C picked up his periscope and thrust one end of it through the hole he had made in the bottom left corner of the window. It had been summer when he had begun to hide in the loft, and the aperture had then admitted warm air. He adjusted the periscope and squatted by it, but looked over it and not through it.

Presently, the man in the dark suiting was seen turning away from the counter. Behind the counter, G. F. Watt leant forward with both arms on the counter and hands clasped, watching his customer leave. The customer came through the door of the café, into the comparative darkness of the street. As he came, he tucked a small pink carton into one of his jacket pockets. While he was crossing the road, nearing the point where C would no longer be able to see him, C put his eye to the lower mirror of the periscope.

In the arrangement of mirrors, the man in the dark suiting became visible in attenuated form. A flaw in one of the mirrors rendered him very tall and thin, while a blurry effect covered his head, so that he appeared to have a sharp face covered with flesh-coloured fur. The side of the house was represented obliquely, with the distortion of perspective. The long legs of the man climbed up two steep stone steps. The man vanished through a slot in the brickwork.

'If he poisons her, I'll be in there after him. I will. Poor little kitten in there with that snake of a man!'

C was about to bring the periscope from the hole in the garage window, and had already leant back from the window in order to do so, when a movement in the arrangement of mirrors caught his eye. He bent his head to the instrument again.

In the steep perspective of brick visible through the arrangement of mirrors were several niches, the nearer niches being wider than the further niches. A distant and narrow niche could be interpreted by a skilled observer as a brown side gate set in the wall on the far side of the house. Through this niche or slot was stepping a man in a ragged jacket. Because a street lamp stood between the watcher and the ragged man, his face was clearly visible as he looked across the road.

'What's *he* think he's up to?'

The man with the ragged jacket crossed the road. He carried a small white jug in one hand, swinging it in a way that indicated it was empty. C observed him directly through the window of the garage and not through the periscope. As the man entered the café, G. F. Watt could be seen behind the counter, speaking to the man. Watt was obscured as he moved behind the counter, first by his customer and then by an arrangement of packaged goods in one of the windows. Then he could be seen going through a door behind the counter. Stuck to the door was a poster; the details on it could not be seen from the garage.

The owner of the café presently reappeared with a white object that he passed over the counter to his customer. His customer turned away and walked out of the door of the café. The lights from the café shone strongly onto the road now. Little illumination was left in the sky. As the man in the ragged jacket crossed the road, he was observed to be carrying a small white jug of the kind generally used for milk. He carried the jug before him with care, steadying it with both hands. He crossed the road and disappeared from the range of C's view.

'Blighter! I know what he's up to.'

C did not attempt to follow the man's further progress through the periscope. Holding the periscope firmly in in his right hand, he thrust it through the hole in the window, allowing his right hand to pass through also. By turning his wrist, he could adjust the instrument so

171

that it assumed a vertical position and looked over the slope of the metal roof at a section of the house otherwise unavailable to scrutiny.

After some manipulation, he looked through the arrangement of mirrors. Again he had the bow window on the first floor of the house under surveillance. The window was unlit from within. A radiance in the western sky, shining from the back of the house, rendered its details with dull clarity.

In the bow window, the woman with the tawny hair was sitting. She appeared to stare out of the window. She wore a coat. Her arms protruded from the coat. She rested her fists under her high cheek-bones. Now and again her shoulders shook.

C pushed the peaked cap back from his forehead with his left hand. Outside the window, his right hand grew cold.

The woman in the bow window was observed to turn her head as if to listen to a sound behind her. Light came on in the room, very bright and sudden, silhouetting the woman and making features impossible to see. She turned her head away from the light.

A man in dark suiting loomed behind her. His lips were moving as if he were talking to the woman. In his hand he carried a glass. One side of the glass gleamed with reflected light. The glass was about a quarter full of some grey liquid. Suddenly the glass became almost as tall as the man. It disappeared from the watcher's view behind the woman's back, and the woman's head became attenuated, growing narrow and thin.

The man reached out his right hand and put it on the woman's shoulder. The woman turned violently towards him, bringing her hands from her cheeks as she did so. It could be seen that the glass flew in an arc, changing shape as it did so. It was lost beyond the side of the arrangement of mirrors. C flicked his right wrist so that the periscope moved slightly. He saw that the man had stepped back so as almost to be concealed from sight by the bow window. His left shoulder and part of his head were hidden from inspection by the arrangement of mirrors by a curtain hanging in the window. He was brushing at the lapels of his dark suiting. Because the light was behind him, the expression on his face was impossible to see. He stepped forward and put out his right arm which blossomed to strange proportions in the flaw in the mirrors. He struck the woman across the face with his right hand. She threw up her arms and moved swiftly towards him. The man retreated. He became hidden by the side of the bow window. Momentarily, the woman's hair made a long tawny spike as she moved into the room. Then she became hidden from view by the side of the window. Nothing could be seen in the window but light pouring through its panes and wallpaper of an indistinguishable pattern on a further wall.

'Someone ought to do for him.'

The bow window, pouring its light out into the side of the garden, trembled in the arrangement of mirrors. C grunted. Carefully, he brought in his wrist and his right hand clutching the periscope through the gap in the window at the front of the garage. He set the periscope down on the floor below the window. Sitting down beside it, he drew his knees up before him, resting his left hand on his knees and thrusting his right hand under his left armpit to warm.

4

A certain amount of light still lingered in the loft above the garage. Through the square window at the other end of the loft, light came from the brightest part of the sky, A small section of a brick wall could be seen, and a distant tree in another property beyond the garden; beyond that, a troubled band of pink light marked where the sun set behind clouds.

Within the loft, a few simple shapes were visible. On the left of where C sat was a smoothly curved bulk made jagged in the middle (as if it had struck a rock) where a tarpaulin hung over the side of it. One point towards the far end of the smoothly curved surface reflected back the dying light from the window; the reflection trailed into straight lines where individual planks along the hull caught it on their edges. On the other side of the loft, the cartons made a continuous shape, black with five sharp corners, except where the box nearest to C picked up a reflection of light from the windows of the café opposite the front of the house. Along the floor were a number of small wet patches which reflected light from the window at the back of the garage.

Stuck to the side of one of the cartons was a cheap colour reproduction of a once-popular painting. It was possible to discern in the fading light that it represented a symbolic confrontation between the two sexes in which, by inserting certain images, the artist had cast doubt upon both the advisability and the possible success of the confrontation. This ambiguity was further increased by the poor light, which fused the man and woman portrayed into a semi-recumbent whole, in which only the faces of the pair, and of a lamb upon the girl's lap, were really distinguishable.

Setting down the red-and-white striped phone, the President said angrily, 'It's that confounded Holman Hunt picture again, with the shepherd and the heavy-eyed dame and all that stuff. G had it, S had it, now we are told C has it. What does this mean, Baynes, for God's sake?'

The Head of CK5 said, 'We have checked up on Hunt, sir. He was one of our men. Got killed in the Riga affair, eight or nine years ago. You still think this report concerns a place somewhere else on this globe, existing contemporaneously?'

'Get that painting photo-copied, send it out to all agents. We've got to identify the site Hunt pictured and

get men there at once, search every inch of depicted territory—I don't care where it is. The key to the whole business clearly lies there. Move, Baynes!'

The Wandering Virgin continued to report in her singsong voice, so Baynes inclined his head and left the room, walking at a certain speed and closing the door behind him. Outside, four men waited, two of them in uniform and two in grey suits. The two in grey suits turned to Baynes eagerly and asked, 'Any luck, sir?'

Baynes said, 'We're in more trouble, boys. It's Hunt's old secret BMAC site again. Either of you remember the Riga affair?'

Rising, the Suppressor of the Archives lightly touched the Wandering Virgin on the shoulder, so that her voice ceased in the chamber. She sat with her eyes wide, unseeing.

'My apologies to the court,' the Suppressor said. 'The Virgin appears to have lost the report. Precisely—indeed, even imprecisely—who the President and Baynes are will probably remain forever unknown to us. Another time dimension entirely.'

The Impaler rose and gathered his robe about him. 'I believe we have all heard enough to draw our own conclusions, eh?'

Now the light in the loft was dim. C remained as he was for a long while, staring in the general direction of the cartons, on occasions muttering to himself.

'Someone really ought to do for him.'

Changing his position so that he was on his knees, C removed his right hand from his left armpit, flexed it, and picked up the home-made periscope. It was made from six cylindrical tins which gleamed in the dull light. Grasping it in his right hand, C passed the telescope through the hole in the bottom left-hand corner of the window by which he knelt and adjusted it so that it stood upright and the top mirror looked over the slope of the garage roof towards the side of the house, while the bottom mirror faced through the garage window towards him. With his left hand, he adjusted the peaked cap on his head. He looked into the mirror.

By a slight movement of his right hand, a lighted bow window set in the south-east side of the house became partly visible in the arrangement of mirrors. Yellow curtains hung on either side of the window. Through the window, the rear wall of the room could be seen. The wall was papered; the pattern of the wallpaper could not be distinguished. No movement could be seen in the room. From the angle of the shadows cast by the window into the dark beyond, it could be determined that the light in the room did not come from an overhead source. Possibly it came from a light fitting on one of the walls. Nobody was to be seen in the room through the arrangement of mirrors.

C watched through the hole in the window, his gaze fixed on the bottom mirror of his periscope. The brightly lit window of the bedroom revealed nothing but wallpaper, the pattern of which could not be made out.

After some while, C brought his right hand back through the window, clutching the home-made periscope. He tucked it under his left arm, tucking his right hand under the armpit of the left arm. Getting to his stockinged feet, he bent his shoulders and made his way down the

centre of the loft. At the other end, he set the periscope
down on the floor under the square window that looked
over the garden, removed his hand from his armpit,
and took the peaked cap from his head. Crossing to the
nearest of the cardboard boxes, he opened it and dropped
the peaked cap inside.

Turning back to the window that faced onto the garden,
C picked up the periscope. The window was divided into
four sections by two bars; the section at the bottom left
had no glass in it. Cradling the periscope in his hand, C
pushed it through the hole. By manœuvring the periscope into a vertical position, it was possible to see over
the slope of the roof to a part of the south-east side of
the house that otherwise would have been invisible from
the window of the garage.

As C gazed into the lower mirror of the periscope, a
reflection of part of the brickwork of the house came into
view. The dusk made it hardly distinguishable as brickwork. After another slight movement of his hand, a
reflection of a bow window came into view. The movement of the hand steadied.

A light shone from the window. From the window at
the front of the garage, the bow window had been viewed
on its east side; from the window at the back of the
garage, it was viewed on its west side, and from a more
oblique angle. Part of a curtain could be seen in the window, and an indistinguishable blank behind it that was
probably the front wall of the room. No movement
could be seen through the arrangement of mirrors.

'They must still be there. Perhaps he's doing her in.'

A movement in the room could be discerned through
the arrangement of mirrors. A shadow was visible, mov-

ing across the room. It spread across the window. The window went completely dark.

Crouching by the window of the garage, C closed his eyes. After a minute, he reopened them, and again peered at the lower mirror. It took him some while before he could detect the outline of the bow window. It was picked out by the stain of light in the western sky. The illumination from inside the room remained switched off.

C drew the periscope into the loft and placed it below the window. He went over to the square cut in the floor of the loft, in which the top of a wooden ladder glimmered. He climbed down the ladder. The ladder was bolted to the rear wall of the garage, in an upright position. The man descended into the garage. A black car stood on the floor of the garage, occupying most of the space. It showed itself only as a few lines of dull highlight here and there. The smell of the garage was fusty and oily. To one side of the ladder was a door leading to the garden. It was made of light metal. It was closed.

C opened the door and looked out.

A quantity of light still remained in the garden, rendering some of its details in silhouette. Behind the newly opened door, and running away from it in a south-westerly direction, was a high brick wall. It caught a certain tone from the sky, although the top of it, which was armed with shards of broken bottle set into the concrete, being outlined against the sky, appeared entirely black. At its far end, where a sunken garden lay, it merged into a confusion of gloom from which no detail could be discerned until C's eye, sweeping towards the north of the horizon, picked out the clear outlines of apple and plum tree branches against the clouds. Slightly to one side of the trees and seen partly through their branches was an old brick building. The peak of its roof stood plainly above the indistinct mass of land further away and lying behind it. Below the roof, a round window set in the front of the old brick building could be distinguished, for a feeble glimmer of yellow light was emitted from it.

'All right for you, chum! Fat lot you care for anything but yourself. One of these days. . . .'

On C's right hand, the house rose large and dark, cutting off the rest of the garden. The windows showed only a dim reflected light from the sky. The dining-room window appeared to show some illumination not entirely accounted for by the fact that it had two windows, the second one being set round the corner of the house and visible in part through the window near to C. C regarded it for some time.

He did not approach the house. He began to walk slowly, taking his steps one at a time, away from the garage and parallel with the house, keeping his gaze continuously on the window of the dining-room. In this way, he got, step by step, a fuller view of the inside of the room. Nothing inside the room was visible to him but a vague shape, part dark, part dim reflected light, that he judged marked the whereabouts of the top of the dining-room table.

Under his stockinged feet, the grass was wet. Wetness oozed through his stockings. Some light was still cast onto the lawn from the sky. Some flecks of a white material lay about C's feet. Looking down, he identified a number of pigeon feathers.

It was now possible to see that light was shining into the dining-room. In the corner of the room furthest away from the windows, a door was set. This door was half open. Light shone through the door from a source beyond it. From where C stood on the lawn, amid the pigeon feathers, he could see through the half open door into a hallway. In the hallway, little could be seen; a plain carpet of a crimson colour, and a length of panelled wall, against which stood a chest made of dark wood. One end of the chest was hidden by the edge of the door. On the wall above the chest, a framed picture hung. There was a good deal of red in the picture, but its subject could not be distinguished. There was no movement in the hall. C's ears could detect no sound within the house.

The sky grew duller, until all parts of it were the same sombre tone. The garden became almost completely dark. Only the ragged edge of the wall on one side and the sharp lines of the house on the other, together with the feeble glimmer of yellow light from the old brick building, stood out from the general obscurity. From the house came no sound or movement.

Walking on a course parallel to the house, C returned to the garage. The door in the back wall of the garage was ajar. He pulled it further open and went in. He shut the door behind him.

Inside the garage, the black car seemed to absorb light. C stood with his left hand holding one of the rungs of an upright ladder bolted into the rear wall of the garage. He bent his left leg in order to raise the left foot, which he clasped with his right hand. The sock and the foot within it were wet and cold. After a short while, he held onto the rung of the upright ladder with his right hand and bent his right leg so that he could clasp his right foot with his left hand. The foot and the sock that covered it were wet and cold.

C put both feet onto the concrete of the garage floor and stood clasping the rung of the upright ladder with both hands.

He turned away from the ladder. Using his hands to feel for obstacles, he made his way round the car. By the rear tyre, his right foot trod in a puddle on the floor. Keeping the south-east wall of the garage at his back, he got to the front of the garage. Two doors stood at the front of the garage, secured by a modern lock of a tumbler type. One of the two doors, the one further from the house, was additionally secured in place by two long bolts, one at the top and one at the bottom of the door. C moved to the other door and worked the knob on the tumbler lock. He pushed the door open slightly and secured the lock with a small lever so that it could not fall back into place until the lever was released. He slid out between the doors.

Standing on the pavement, C looked up and down a road. On his left was the bulk of the house, its front glancingly illuminated by a street lamp that stood beyond it. On his right, some paces distant, was another street lamp, and beyond it others which, due to the effect of perspective, appeared to be placed more and more closely together. They could be seen to lead to a jumble of lights, some of which defined a shadowy line of pillars that marked a railway station. A car moved up the road from the direction of the railway station. It contained four men; all sat with their hands over their eyes. C waited till the car had passed.

On the other side of the road was a café, the double windows of which were illuminated. Various goods could be seen displayed in the windows of the café. In the window on the left, C could detect a table marked by a red and white squared cloth that covered it.

C crossed the road to the café, opened one of the double doors, and walked in. He turned to the left and approached the table he had seen through the window. At the table stood a wooden chair of the folding variety. C pulled the chair seat from under the table and sat down. He blinked his eyes.

Behind the counter, a man leaned. His arms lay across the counter; his hands were interlinked. C signalled to him. The man nodded, and went to a door set in the wall behind the counter. He went through the door, closing it behind him. On the door was stuck a poster advertising a circus that had visited the town some weeks previously.

Next to the closed door were shelves on which had been arranged several brands of cigarettes. Rising from the chair on which he sat, C moved over to the counter, leant over it, extended his right hand, and took a packet containing ten cigarettes from the shelf. Returning to the table, pocketing the cigarettes as he did so, he sat down on the hard wooden seat.

When he had rested his elbows on the table-top, he leaned forward and peered through the window at the front of the house.

The front of the house had been designed with rules of symmetry in mind. The window on one side of the front door was balanced by the window on the other side of the front door. C looked at the window to the right of the front door. This belonged to the sitting-room. A light burned in the sitting-room. Thick curtains had been drawn across the window; a slight gap had been left between the curtains, a gap slightly wider at the top than lower down, as if the curtains had been drawn in haste.

Behind the counter of the café, a door opened and a man entered, bearing in his left hand a cup and saucer with a spoon in the saucer. He brought these round to the front of the shop and set them down on the table at which C sat. The table was covered with a cloth patterned in red and white squares.

Taking hold of the spoon, C began to stir the liquid in the cup, looking up at the man as he did so.

'Been busy?'

'How do you mean?'

'Many people in?'

'I'll be closing soon. There's a strike up at the car factory.'

'Seen anything going on over the road?'

'The men won't go back till they get better conditions.'

'Is that so? Have you seen her just lately?'

'I've been busy. You're wasting your time with her.'

'So they tell me. He'll do something he shouldn't to her, one of these days.'

'So they tell me. Myself, I wouldn't blame him. She's a proper little cat.'

'Have you seen her since he came over here last?'

'How do you mean exactly? How's the coffee? You haven't tasted it yet.'

'Have you caught sight of her in the last few minutes?'

'I tell you you're wasting your time with her. I saw her draw her sitting-room curtains just now, if that's any help to you. Is that what you wanted to know?'

C lifted the cup of coffee to his lips and sipped it. G. F. Watt rested his hands on the back of the folding chair and gazed out through the café window. C found the coffee was not hot. He drained the coffee and set the cup back empty in its saucer.

'That's nice coffee. You're about to close, I suppose.'

'It gets dark these evenings, doesn't it? Was that what you wanted to know?'

'You're not kidding it was what I wanted to know.'

'How do you mean I was not kidding? I wasn't kidding. I saw her draw the curtains, I tell you. He said she was upset.'

'She'll get over it. Pet pigeon died. Thanks for the coffee.'

'Did you like it? He didn't mention the pigeon. He doesn't say much, not to speak of, like when the baby died.'

'Very nice—nice and sweet. I'd better get back. Thanks a lot.'

'I fancy a cup myself, seeing you. . . .'

Pushing the table forward, C rose. He winked at the man, went to the door, opened it, and walked out onto the pavement in his stockinged feet. A man passed him, rolling a rusty bicycle wheel along like a hoop. No traffic passed on the road. C crossed the road, making for a concrete and asbestos garage that stood next to the house, separated from the house by a metre and a half of brick wall. The door of the garage stood ajar. C slipped through the opening into the darkness of the garage.

Turning, he pulled the garage door shut and pressed down a small lever on the mechanism of the lock. He heard the lock click.

Domoladossa went home to his wife that evening in a preoccupied fashion. He was trying to puzzle out the events in Mr. Mary's house—and to puzzle out, incidentally, how the events were interfered with by reason of their being observed.

Others, too, felt the sense of mystery. Corless sat alone on the hillside, guarding the manifestation, in hourly anxiety in case it went away as suddenly as it had come. Joe Growleth packed up before the usual late afternoon rush to New Jersey began, but throughout an evening spent with his two wives, Peggy so charmingly white, Sophie so charmingly black, he remained preoccupied. The two men took the little boy home but phoned the police and then wondered if they had done the right thing.

And there were watchers watching them, and they too had watchers, who also had watchers, and so on, and so on, in an almost infinite series. Every stage of watcher had a theory about the watched; every stage put something of its own passions into the watching.

Sitting quiet in her own room, the fingertips of one hand resting in her tawny hair, Mr. Mary's wife sat at her own screen and regarded the cycle of universes as night closed in.

The interior of the garage was almost entirely obliterated by dark. The bulk of the car seemed to breathe out darkness. Only at the far end of the chamber did a blur of greyness appear, filtering down from the square window set in the loft. C stood and listened before he moved forward, feeling his way along the side of the car between the car and the south-east wall of the garage. He trod carefully, so as to avoid any puddles on the concrete floor. At the far end of the garage, he saw the skeletal shape of a wooden ladder, bolted upright against the wall and leading to a loft above the garage. He climbed the ladder and scrambled into the loft.

A square window was set in the wall by the top of the ladder. It was divided into four smaller squares, only three of which were glazed. Cold air blew through the unglazed square. Through one of the quarters of the window a cool breeze blew. C inserted a wet cube of wood into the gap.

Walking with his shoulders stooped, C proceeded to the other end of the loft. A square window overlooked the road. The window was divided into quarters, one quarter of which was unglazed; a cool air blew through it. Feeling on the floor below the window, C brushed with his fingers a cube of wood, which he picked up and inserted into the gap in the window. As he did so, he glanced out of the window. Across the road was a café with double windows. Lights shining through the windows lit the wide pavement outside. Through one of the windows could be seen a square table with a red and white squared cloth. The back of a chair protruded behind the table. Resting his hands on the back of this chair was a man; he stood there with shoulders slumped, looking through the window at the house opposite.

C turned away from the window. Along one side of

the loft ran the dark shape of a canoe. Its hull reflected the light from the window in a blur. A tarpaulin lay across the boat. When he had pulled the tarpaulin off the boat onto the floor, C climbed into the boat and lay down in it. The seats had been removed from the boat and the well of it partly filled with wood shavings and blankets. C settled himself on top of the blankets, propping himself up on one elbow.

He felt in his right-hand trouser pocket, extracting a packet of cigarettes. He tore off the wrapping of the packet and threw the paper onto the floor. Opening the packet, he extracted one cigarette, sniffed it, and put one end of it between his lips. Having tucked the packet down beside him against the side of the canoe, he slid open the little drawer of his box of matches, selected one, and struck it on the side of the box.

As he lit the cigarette with it, the flame illuminated a very small picture stuck to the roof above C's head. C cast his glance upwards at the picture. It was a coloured card found in a packet of tea, one of a series of twenty-four entitled Wonders of Nature. It depicted two snakes. One snake had caught the tail of the other in its mouth. At the same time, the second snake had part of the tail of the first snake down its gullet. The two snakes lay in a circle, their eyes gleaming; they were swallowing each other. C blew out a cloud of smoke at them.

He shook the match. Its burning end turned black, the flame faded and died. For a moment, a spark of red gleamed just beyond C's fingers, then it also died. C threw the match down onto the floor of the loft. He leant against the crumpled blankets, propped on his left elbow. The end of his cigarette glowed more brightly when he inhaled its smoke.

The square window set in the rear wall of the loft slightly alleviated the darkness in which he lay. He looked through it as he smoked. The garden presented itself as a formless total blackness, from which the peak of an old building was raised, distinguishable against the lighter darkness of the clouds in the night sky. Below the peak of the building, punctuating the blackness of the garden, a glimmer of yellow light showed.

C continued to smoke the cigarette until it burnt his fingers. Without hurry, he leant over the side of the canoe and squashed out the stub of cigarette against the floor. He brushed his fingers together. He resumed his former position, lying back and propping himself on his left elbow. He let his head roll sideways until it rested against the metal of the roof, yawned, and continued to stare out through the window at the blackness of the garden.

Rainclouds drew over the sky, darkening it still further, until the peaked outline of an old nearby coach house was lost. A glimmer of yellow light, feebly showing in that direction, winked and was extinguished. C yawned again and continued still to gaze through the window at the blackness of the garden.

Forgetting his flock, the youth leant forward, so that her sturdy form touched his chest and arms. As she half-turned, her hair was against his cheek. He could smell the warmth of it and the scents of her body, which the sunny day released.

189

Nobody was near. The sheep could take care of themselves. Within his imprisoning hand, he could feel the doomed moth flutter. Her hand was raised towards it in a gesture of indecision.

She waited.

He waited.

Oxford, July 1967